Lucinda looked up to see Edward's cool gray eyes studying her with detached interest, and she caught her breath a little. She discovered in that moment that she had not forgotten anything about him.

He was the same cool young man who had refused to be impressed by her schoolgirl wickedness, just as he appeared to be quite unimpressed now by her transformation into a young lady of fashion. She was annoyed to feel the old hero worship touch her briefly as she acknowledged him in her curtsey to his family.

"Edward Chevening," she thought wryly as the housekeeper showed her to her room. "A second son!"

Fawcett Crest Books
by Mary Ann Gibbs:

THE ADMIRAL'S LADY   23678-1 $1.50

THE APOTHECARY'S DAUGHTER   23649-8 $1.75

THE GLASS PALACE   23063-5 $1.50

HORATIA   23175-5 $1.50

A MOST ROMANTIC CITY   23300-6 $1.50

THE ROMANTIC FRENCHMAN   P2869 $1.25

THE TEMPESTUOUS PETTICOAT   23489-4 $1.50

A YOUNG LADY OF FASHION   23843-1 $1.75

A Young Lady of Fashion

MARY ANN GIBBS

FAWCETT CREST • NEW YORK

A YOUNG LADY OF FASHION

Published by Fawcett Crest Books, a unit of CBS Publications, the Consumer Publishing Division of CBS Inc.

Copyright © 1978 by Mary Ann Gibbs

ALL RIGHTS RESERVED

ISBN: 0-449-23843-1

All the characters in this book are fictitious, and any resemblance to actual persons living or dead is purely coincidental.

Printed in the United States of America

10 9 8 7 6 5 4 3 2 1

A Young Lady
of Fashion

One

Edgecombe Manor, five miles outside Bath, was the favorite home of Sir William and Lady Chevening and their family. Their visits to Chevening Place, the family seat in Kent with its twenty thousand acres, took place only in the summer months while Sir William's father lived, and were curtailed even more when old Lady Chevening ruled there alone.

Edgecombe, left to Sir William by an old uncle of his mother's, had been built in the reign of Elizabeth. It was of Tudor red brick, mellowed to rose color with the years, its chimneys were tall and twisted, its windows stiff bays. It was built naturally in the shape of an E, with wings on either side and a porch in the middle, where a massive door led directly into a stone-flagged hall, its paneled walls and the sturdy staircase that led from it being black with age.

The wall opposite to the entrance held a wide fireplace,

its stone chimney breast ornamented with the crest and coat of arms of old Lady Chevening's family. The hearth accommodated great logs, blazing in the winter with a cheerful welcome and kept on hot ash in the summer so that on cool evenings a leather bellows would send them crackling again. The hall expressed the atmosphere of the little manor house: it was warm and cheerful and the rooms were small and cozy. Twenty couples dancing in a drawing room would constitute a ball, whereas in the smallest of the drawing rooms at Chevening forty guests would have been scarcely enough for a musical evening.

Lucinda Crayne's first visit to Edgecombe was in the spring of 1821, when she was eighteen. She had been invited there with her brother Frank, who was a friend of Edward Chevening, the second son, and from the first moment she saw the manor she fell in love with it, with its paved courtyard and red walls and the gray gables where the lichen grew in patches. She loved too the informal gardens that surrounded it and the welcoming rooms and cheerful fires. Above all, she delighted in the gay company of the young people there and their friends, a contrast indeed to the bleak isolation of Crayne Castle in Buckinghamshire where she lived with her uncle, Lord Crayne. Crayne Castle was almost larger and certainly a great deal colder than Chevening Place.

There were five in the Chevening family, three sons and two daughters. Vincent, the eldest, was twenty-five and spent most of his time in London; Edward was Frank's age, twenty-two, and Jasper at nineteen held a cornetcy in the 14th Light Dragoons. The girls, Maria, aged sixteen, and Liz, fifteen, were the youngest.

"I remember Edward," Lucinda said as she discussed

the family with her brother on their journey from Buckinghamshire. "Although he had no eyes for a gawky schoolgirl when he last visited Crayne."

"The gawky girl having developed into a young lady of fashion since then," Frank told her, smiling, "I daresay he may have eyes for her now."

She stroked her green velvet pelisse with a hand gloved in French kid, and under her silk bonnet, with the white ostrich feather curling round its crown, her dark eyes were thoughtful. She was remembering the thin-faced, serious young man who had come to Crayne to talk books and art with her uncle and Frank. When she had tried to draw his attention to herself with some outrageous remark that drew a stern rebuke from her uncle he had scarcely raised an eyebrow. He had merely smiled and said she reminded him of his sisters.

His sisters indeed! She dismissed Edward Chevening and changed the subject to her uncle. "When I went to say goodbye to him before we left," she told her brother, "he said that with the brilliant summer that my Aunt Winter had planned for me he would be extremely surprised if I did not secure a title and a fortune by the end of it. I hope I shall not disappoint him though I scolded him for his cynicism. I asked if he thought happiness had nothing to do with marriage and he said that most women found it easily enough, given plenty of jewels and carriages and pretty clothes. It is a curious attitude for a man whose own marriage was so happy."

"Perhaps it is because his wife died after only a year that he has set his face against a similar tragedy where you and I are concerned, my dear."

She slipped a hand into his arm and asked if Vincent

Chevening would be there. "I understand he is the real charmer of the family," she added.

Frank said that the country bored Vincent Chevening at that time of year, and he was seldom seen out of London. "But I promise you he will be there in spirit."

"Now what do you mean by that?"

"I mean that you will hear of little else but Vincent during our stay. He will be talked of with pride by every member of the family—except perhaps little Liz, who adores Edward, strangely enough. You will be told by the rest that he is the best rider in the county, and the best driver of cattle—which is a black lie, because I have seldom seen a worse—that he is clever, which also is not true, because in some things he is deplorably stupid. You will hear how much everyone admires him, and I will admit that he has good looks and great charm of manner. But if any other man is praised for some activity— Edward, for instance, or Jasper, or any of their friends— it will be capped at once by the information that nobody can hold a candle to Vincent. He rules his family when he is absent as easily as he does when he is with them. They have set him up on a pedestal and nobody is allowed to rock it."

Lucinda glanced at her brother with a smile. "May I conclude, my dearest Frank, that you do not like Sir William's heir?"

"I neither like nor dislike him. I am only angry for the way he imposes on Edward's good nature. Edward is one of the best fellows alive."

"He will not do for me. Uncle Herbert was insistent that I should not consider second sons. 'The heir or nothing,' he said."

"I am sure he said nothing of the sort. You are in a

teasing mood, Lucinda. The fact is that Edward's family find him too bookish. Edgecombe is in the midst of open country, where there is game to shoot and there are foxes to hunt and hares to course and a trout stream in the valley beneath the house—it stands on a hill—and Sir William and his friends enjoy this kind of life, as I do myself. Edward shocked them all years ago by saying he could see no advantage in killing creatures simply to prove that you were a better shot than your neighbors."

"Is he not a good shot?"

"First class. He is also an excellent rider and he enjoys foxhunting, but I daresay that is because Master Reynard often gets away. On a wet day, though, when the rest of the men of a house party are playing cards or billiards or are in the gun room experimenting with the tying of flies, you will find him in the library poring over books. And Liz will invariably be with him, curled up in a window seat and lost in some dry book of travel that he has found to keep her quiet. The family call her his shadow, and Lady Chevening says he encourages her in tastes that are the despair of her governesses."

"I was the despair of *my* governesses," said Lucinda. "At least I always thought that was why they left Crayne so frequently, but the pretty ones may have left for some reason to do with Uncle Herbert." Her eyes met her brother's demurely and he laughed.

"He certainly seemed to be relieved when the last of them—if I remember rightly a plain and elderly dragon of a lady—advised him to send you to boarding school. Are you glad to be finished with it, my love?"

She made a little face. "I was sorry to part with the friends I made there, but I am afraid I did not behave very well. My deportment was said to be deplorable, my needlework worse, and the only thing at which I excelled was dancing. But when I told Uncle Herbert I would like to dance on a stage in a theater he was shocked. 'What,' he said, 'and show your legs to the world! That would not be the act of a lady, Lucinda!' I protested that I had not ugly legs, and he replied, that on the contrary they were very pretty ones—he can turn a neat compliment when he chooses—and then he must spoil it by saying, 'But you show too much of them.' So I hastily pulled down my skirts and fetched my embroidery and worked on it the whole morning instead of reading the *Times* to him, which made him very cross."

"How you do tease the poor fellow," said Frank. "I would not dare take the liberties with him that you do."

"He astonishes me by his prudery," said his sister. "When you and I are fully aware of what goes on in that horrid house of his in Brighton and where his Paris visits lead him, I wonder he dares to scold me about showing my legs."

"He was not scolding you," said Frank consolingly. "He has strict notions on what a Crayne female should or should not do. She must be above reproach."

"A case of *noblesse oblige,*" sniffed Lucinda, nose in air.

"Something of the sort." He smiled at her affectionately. There were four years between them and he was very fond of his wayward younger sister. "Are you warm enough? It is cold in this carriage, and the foot-warmer has lost its heat."

"Carriages are always cold, but my pelisse is warm." The long coat was lined with fur from neck to hem, and the matching dress beneath it had a broad band of the same fur at the bottom. The dress was of a thick corded silk known to ladies of fashion as *gros de Naples*, and although younger ladies affected to find it warm enough for winter wear, their mothers and aunts preferred merino for their dresses, in dark colors, brightening them with colored ribbons.

The countryside was becoming more hilly and wooded now in the late sunshine of the March afternoon, and their journey would soon be at an end.

"I am longing to meet your beloved Chevenings," she said, "all five of them, if Vincent is there."

"Six," he corrected her. "I forgot to mention Miss Wakefield."

"Who is she?"

"I suppose she is a relative of sorts. Her stepmother was Sir William's youngest sister who met Amos Wakefield, a Yorkshireman, at a ball in London and fell in love with him. He was a widower with one child, Sarah, to whom the second Mrs. Wakefield became much attached. Her husband built a country house for her in Kent, five miles from Chevening Place, and Sarah was taken to play with the young Chevenings when they were visiting their grandparents. Her father contracted a bad chill one winter's day while out shooting, and died of it, and his wife did not survive him more than a few months. As Sarah was the same age as Maria, old Lady Chevening suggested she should make her home at Edgecombe Manor."

"Is she pretty?"

He laughed. "She is the dumpiest little creature you ever saw, with a sharp way of saying things that must come from her Yorkshire forebears. But she has one great attraction that even Maria, handsome as she is, has not. She is heiress to one hundred thousand pounds."

"Frank!" Lucinda gazed at her brother in astonishment. "Can there be so much money in the world?" Their uncle kept the young people deplorably short of cash. "Well, of course you must marry her. You know Uncle Herbert is always urging you to marry as you are the last of the line. Only think what one hundred thousand pounds would do for poor old Crayne!"

"And only think what marriage to Miss Wakefield would do for me," said her brother unkindly. "I am sorry, Lucinda, but not even for Uncle Herbert's sake will I enter for the Wakefield stakes."

"Is Vincent Chevening in for them?"

"He may well be next year when Miss Wakefield and Maria Chevening have their coming-out ball in London. It will depend, I daresay, on how deeply he is in debt."

"I thought he inherited a fortune when he came of age?"

"He came in for sixty thousand pounds or so, I believe, but that was four years ago and I shall be surprised if there is much of it left by this time. He visits White's nearly every night—a club I have never entered. Jasper does not patronize it either, although there is an excuse for him as he holds a commission in a crack regiment. He and I prefer to part with more modest sums in backing our favorite champions of the Ring; we both enjoy a good mill."

"And does Edward enjoy mills?"

"When he is in London I can sometimes persuade him to accompany us, if there is a meeting at Richmond or Moulsey or the Common at Wimbledon—somewhere near enough to tempt him. But he usually leaves after the twentieth round or so, if the claret flows too freely."

"I daresay he thinks there is little point in a crowd of

gentlemen standing round a ring to watch two grown men pound each other to pulp."

"Those are his sentiments exactly."

A turning in the Bath road suddenly revealed the city itself, a veritable queen among cities, standing up in all its white beauty against the green of the English countryside. At such a distance it was possible to forget its hilly streets where invalids made their way to and from the waters and where ladies walked demurely, tempted by the shops; to ignore the existence of the Upper Rooms, where balls took place with such decorum that it was hard to believe that Bath was reputed to be more depraved than London itself. A beauty with her morals tucked out of sight, she displayed herself for all the world to see and admire, as Lucinda was admiring her now. And then a turning in the road presented itself and the carriage left the Bath road and made a final leisurely way to Edgecomble on its wooded hill.

Sir William was away, having some business to attend to in London, and Lady Chevening, a statuesque lady in black velvet, was there with her family to give the travelers a warm welcome.

"We slept last night at Oxford," Lucinda told her hostess. "Although it is not true to say that we *slept* there because there must be a thousand and one clocks in that city, all striking the quarter hour one after another. I do not know how anybody can sleep or study there."

"One becomes accustomed to it," said a voice beside her, and she looked up to see Edward's cool gray eyes studying her with detached interest. She caught her breath a little and discovered in that moment that she had not forgotten anything about him: his thin aristocratic features might be a little more pronounced, and his thick dark hair might be thicker, and he had grown a pair of side whiskers to pay lip-service to fashion.

But he was the same cool young man who had refused to be impressed by her schoolgirl wickedness, just as he appeared to be quite unimpressed now by her transformation into a young lady of fashion, and she was annoyed to feel the old hero-worship touch her briefly as she acknowledged him in her curtsy to his family.

"Edward Chevening," she thought wryly as the housekeeper showed her to her room. "A second son!"

But she was not the first person who found it difficult to be contemptuous when thinking of Edward Chevening.

Two

Old Merrydew, who used to be Lucinda's nurse and was now her maid, was strict about her resting after the day's journey while she unpacked. When she thought Lucinda was sufficiently recovered, she changed the fur-trimmed traveling dress for one of white sarcenet with a sash the color of copper. She replaited Lucinda's chestnut hair into a coronet on top of her head, securing it with a topaz ornament and brushing the side curls round her old fingers until they lay shining on her charge's shoulders.

The high-waisted dresses of the Regency still persisted in the fashions of that year, flounces at the bottom of the skirts lending them extra weight so that they hung straight and without a crease. The white dress emphasized the slenderness of Lucinda's figure and the shapeliness of her neck and arms, and Merrydew clasped a string of topaz round her neck and put topaz earrings in her ears, the jewels being a birthday gift from her uncle, Lord Crayne.

A tiny beaded reticule was then put into Lucinda's hand, because in those long straight dresses there was no room for pockets, and white satin slippers were fitted to her feet. Only when Merrydew was perfectly satisfied was she allowed to go downstairs to join the family waiting in the drawing room to be summoned to dinner.

She found herself between Jasper and Edward at dinner, and as Jasper started telling Frank the details of a steeplechase in which he had taken part that morning, she turned to her more silent companion.

"So you know Oxford?" she said.

"I had three years at Magdalen," he told her. "My father was apprehensive lest I should become a don, but he was soon reassured: I was far too stupid. I enjoyed my years there nevertheless." His eyes were studying her with the same detachment and did not reveal the interest she had aroused in him. Recollecting the fourteen-year-old tomboy of the schoolroom that he had met at Crayne some years before, he was more surprised and intrigued than she knew by her metamorphosis. She was a pretty creature, even after a long journey: her dark eyes with their long curling lashes were as bright as Maria's, her curls framed a particularly charming face, and she had not yet acquired the affected manners that spoiled so many of the fashionable young ladies he met in London.

It was at this point in his thoughts that Maria addressed Lucinda across her brother. "Do not let Edward start telling you about his 'collection,' " she warned her. "If you do not take care he will bore you with it by the hour. He began it when he was on a visit to Paris one summer and he has thought of little else ever since. It is housed in one of our smallest attics under the roof, and it consists of six pictures, all very dirty, three dull vases and a small bronze horse."

"It is an enchanting little horse." Liz defended her beloved Edward stoutly. "And one of the paintings is a Raphael, Miss Crayne."

"A Raphael?" Lucinda turned startled eyes on her neighbor and saw him flush faintly before he replied with a smile that his sisters talked a great deal of nonsense.

Lucinda ate her fish thoughtfully and said that her mother's brother, Sir Berkeley Winter, had an interesting collection. "I have never found myself bored with it," she added, "and if you should be in London this summer, Mr. Chevening, I must arrange for you to see it. My uncle and aunt are entertaining me in their house in Manchester Square for my first London season."

He replied that few people could have failed to have heard of Sir Berkeley Winter's collection and that he would be most grateful to see it for himself. And then her attention was claimed by Jasper inquiring into the amount of game that had been slaughtered on the Crayne estates the previous autumn and what the prospects were for trout fishing during the summer months.

She told him that he should apply to her brother. "While as for fishing," she added, "we have no trout streams of our own and Uncle Herbert always visits more fortunate friends when the season begins. He is a keen fisherman." Jasper having lost interest in her with this account of the sporting facilities at Crayne, she turned back to his brother and told him that she envied him for his family circle. "Frank and I are the last of the Craynes, but my mother was one of fifteen, and I am handed about from uncle to aunt, and from aunt to uncle, as if I were an express letter sent from one county to the next. When I am not at Crayne most of my time is spent in this way, while Frank hugs himself in his rooms in Manchester Street, just round the corner from Manchester Square. Frank loves London, and will not even admit that its smells too much."

"It can be far from salubrious when the wind is blowing off the river," he agreed. "Although I too enjoy living in London, and if I had my way I would live nowhere else."

"I suppose you belong to some of the more exclusive clubs?" she said.

"On the contrary I do not belong to one."

"Then how do you spend your days when you are there?"

"In watching cargoes from the East being handled on the wharves, in exploring old houses and old churches, making a note of inscriptions carved in stone, in visiting galleries and museums and attending lectures on scientific matters, none of which I am afraid would appeal to a young lady."

She did not know what to make of him and gave her attention to Jasper for the rest of the meal.

There came a spell of mild spring weather when the whole party went riding and Lucinda noticed how careful Edward was of his youngest sister, making sure that she had the quietest mount and riding close to her while they were out. She liked him for it but she wished she could penetrate the coolness that persisted even when neighbors came in to play cards and to dance, most of them jolly country squires with comely gossipy wives, and children of the same age as the young Chevenings. Lucinda found it a delightful form of enjoyment, after the few visitors they saw at Crayne and although Vincent was not there, Jasper had brought with him all the latest dances from London. Lucinda was happy to learn from him and proved an apt pupil, but she wished she could persuade Edward to stand up with her. This, alas, was beyond her powers: Edward, she was told, did not dance.

However, one morning before she went walking with the others he did offer to show her the few treasures that Maria had called his collection. They mounted gravely to the attic where it was housed, followed by Liz skipping from stair to stair behind them, and directly they entered the little room under the roof she saw that here was his interest and the love of his life.

On a shelf near the door were the three little vases of which Maria had spoken so contemptuously. "These are of rock crystal, are they not?" she said, taking them up carefully.

"Yes. The mount of the one you are holding is of silver, the others are silver-gilt, and gold. They were being sold with the effects of a gentleman who had recently died, in a large house near Bath, and I rode out there to examine the lots that were for sale. I had not much money to spend and I was delighted when I had these knocked down to me for seven pounds."

"Are they French?"

"No, Chinese."

"And that picture? Surely it is by Canaletto?"

"Yes. It is of Westminster Bridge and I liked its life and movement, though pictures by Canaletto are not popular because the brown varnish turns them so dark. They go for a song."

"And so you sang your song and got your picture?" she said lightly. She took up a little bronze horse, which

he told her had come from the same house as the vases
and was Chinese in origin.

"This is charming. He is just like my Rascal at Crayne.
His mane flies out in the same way and his tail has the
same twist."

She was then required to express an opinion on the
Raphael.

"I happened to pass one of those secondhand shops in
Paris," he said, "where old garments are hung out to air
in the street, and behind a piece of tapestry in the dirty
window I saw a small picture of a dark-haired madonna.
I went into the shop and asked if I might have a closer
look at it; the shopkeeper was surly and unwilling to
oblige but an English sovereign persuaded him and on a
closer inspection I saw at once that it might be of the same
age as Raphael's paintings. The pigment was the same,
but it might have been done by a student in his workshop
or perhaps a copy of a detail from one of his works by a
contemporary. In any case it charmed me sufficiently to
coax another two sovereigns from my pocket, and that
was the start of my desire to form a collection of my own.
But as you see I have not progressed very far."

"My uncle would be interested to see your madonna
all the same," she said. "It is very like one that he bought
from the Orleans Collection many years ago. I remember
him saying that Raphael painted many madonnas. You
must talk to him about it."

"I will look forward to it," he replied gravely, and then
they heard Maria calling Lucinda and the light died in his
eyes. "You will have to go," he said, and she was disappointed because he made no effort to persuade her to stay.

She became increasingly impatient with him during the
rest of her visit. He seemed content to stay in the back-

ground, living under the shadow of Vincent and outshone even by Jasper. But in spite of his restrained manner she felt that in a time of crisis it would be Edward to whom his family would turn for help.

Their last day at Edgecombe was wet and miserable and during the morning Lucinda visited the library to request Edward to join her brother and Jasper in the billiard room, and to fetch Liz to the drawing room for Pope Joan. "I have been sent for you both," she told them smiling. "And I am not to be denied." She came closer to the library table. "What is your book, Edward? *The Life and Times of Murillo.* It looks dull."

"I find it interesting." He had risen to his feet at her entrance and stood there studying her gravely. She wished she dare tease him but she could find nothing to say and she walked to the window seat where Liz was sitting with a large volume on her lap.

"*Hawkesworth's Voyages!*" she exclaimed. "Great heavens, that is a vast work for a young girl like you!"

"I love adventure stories," said Liz. "True ones, I mean. This book is about the voyages of Captain Cook."

"But have you no books in your schoolroom?"

"Only Sandford and Merton and Mrs. Edgeworth's tales about good children and the dreadful things that happen to those that are bad. I do not find them very elevating."

"I am sure you do not. I hated them." She perched herself on the arm of a chair and removed one of her pearl earrings that had become loose. "Oh this stupid earring!" she said impatiently. "If I kneel beside you, Liz, do you think you can help me with it?"

"There is no need to do that. Allow me." Edward took the little earring from her while Liz put her book down on the library table and ran off to the drawing room. He fitted it with care into the ear she presented to him. She had very pretty ears.

"You did that," she said when he had finished, "as if you had experience in such things." Her eyes were provocative and she saw a hint of amusement in his face as if he were fully aware of her attempt to flirt with him.

"When one has sisters," he told her equably, "one gains such experience."

"But always with sisters?" she asked, and then without giving him time to reply, "Edward, I want you to promise to come to my ball at Easter. I know you dislike dancing, but you will come, will you not? I warn you I shall not forgive you if you are not there."

"My dear child, nobody, least of all yourself, will know if I am there or not."

"Why do you say that? You do not know what it will be like."

"On the contrary I know exactly what it will be like. All London will be there: there will be such a crush that nobody will be able to breathe and your dress and the Crayne jewels that no doubt you will be wearing that night will only be visible when you take the floor to open the ball. But I have no doubt that you will look extremely beautiful."

She moved away from him impatiently. "I shall look as any young woman of eighteen looks in her first season when she is to be thrown on the marriage market. My Uncle Herbert expects to have some good offers for me, but it would have been simpler had he sent me to Mr. Christie's Great Rooms with a label round my neck telling the world that five thousand pounds is to be my dowry and those looking for more need not bid!" She laughed, but he saw the hint of tears in her eyes and he was quick to make amends.

"I will come," he told her gently, "if you will promise me to stay as you are." In her high-necked blue morning dress and with a brooch of pearls pinned at her throat and matching earrings, she looked as young and childlike as Liz. She would hear a lot of unkind criticism and be required to laugh at wit that could be cruel; she would learn a fine taste in looks and clothes and jewels; and she would learn also that few had an appreciation of morals in the brittle, shallow world into which she was going, and he felt an urge to warn her, to arm her in some way beforehand. "Lucinda," he said, "I beg you not to change. Do not let money and position cloud your judgment."

"Do you think it likely?" she asked, puzzled and a little hurt.

"It is very hard to withstand the persuasion of those who would make you believe that they are your superiors," he said, conscious that he was putting it badly.

"You forget that I shall have Frank to protect me." She still did not understand his sudden concern for her.

"Ah yes, Frank will be there." And as he spoke the door opened and Frank himself came into the room.

"We are waiting for you," he said smiling. "And Lucinda—are you for billiards too?"

"No. There are a snug half-dozen of us waiting to play Pope Joan." She left the two men alone and Edward said quickly: "I am glad to have this chance of speaking to you, Frank. I shall be gone before you leave in the morning." He took a letter from beneath the book on Murillo and slipped it into his coat pocket. "I heard from my father this morning. He wishes to see me in London immediately, and I shall be leaving by the midnight coach from Bath tonight."

"Tonight?" Frank was surprised. "Does he give any reason for it?"

"None. But I can guess what it is."

"Vincent?"

"I fear so. I am not mentioning it to the family. I shall tell my mother that I am leaving for London because a paper is being read at the Royal Society tomorrow night on the superior claims of oil-fired gas over that of coal."

"Are you interested in the subject?"

"Not a whit. But it will serve as well as another and Mamma will dismiss my sudden departure as one of my eccentricities." He took his friend's arm. "And now let us attend to our billiards."

As they drove away the following morning Lucinda said she was sorry Edward had gone without giving her the opportunity of saying goodbye.

"Oh," said her brother, smiling, "does the wind sit in that quarter?"

"It does not." She was indignant. "But I think it is a great pity that he is not the eldest of the family instead of that horrid Vincent. I am tired of hearing him talked of as if nothing he does or says is wrong. Lady Chevening even speaks of his debts as if they are but the rashness of youth and will pass in time. Like pimples."

"Yes, he is nearly twenty-six and should have even grown out of pimples by this time. But if Edward had been the eldest may I ask what difference it would have made to my worldly little sister?"

"I should never have left him alone until he had offered for me." Lucinda added complacently, "You may smile, but Uncle Herbert says that I have a great deal of personal charm when I set my mind to it."

"In that case, Uncle Herbert's opinions are of little value and very bad for you," said Frank.

Three

    Sir William Chevening's London house was a mansion in St. James's Square, designed by one of the great architects of the previous century. Under the porch, upheld by pillars, double doors opened into a square hall paved with black and white marble, and from this an archway led to a larger hall where a wide staircase rose on shallow marble treads to a gallery above. On one side of this gallery was a ballroom large enough to accommodate five hundred guests, and on the other side a state drawing room led into a smaller one, both with French Aubusson carpets and furnished in the French style with delicate marquetry, gilded settees and chairs upholstered in rose brocade. The smaller drawing room was especially welcome to ladies overcome with the heat of the ballroom or desiring a little scandalous conversation with a friend.

The paneled staircase was decorated with great carved swags of fruits and flowers, and similar carvings ornamented the walls of the ballroom between long mirrors that reflected the glittering glass chandeliers, suspended from the whole length of a ceiling painted with dancing nymphs and cherubs holding wreathes of flowers.

Above this floor were the bedrooms, dressing rooms and private sitting rooms of the members of the family and their guests. Below it on the ground floor there was a state dining room with a table large enough to seat fifty or more and a side table over ten feet long designed especially for the room by Mr. Chippendale himself. There was also a library leading into Sir William's dressing room where he interviewed his steward and his man of business, a small staircase leading up from it to what had been a powder closet in the old days and now was his dressing room-proper. There was besides on this floor a music room, its ceiling painted with musical instruments and ribbons, a smaller dining room and a breakfast room looking on to a paved courtyard. The far end of this yard formed the back of the coach-houses and stables, the grooms' quarters and the house laundry, approached by a small road at the back of the square.

It was a fine house, and one of which Sir William was justly proud. It spelled wealth and an unassailable position in the land, which, until the day when he sent so peremptorily for his second son, it had seemed nothing could destroy in his lifetime.

On the morning after Edward's arrival Sir William's man of business, Mr. Brayford, had been to see him again. The lawyer was by nature pessimistic, his temperament not at all lightened by the depravity of human nature that he saw around him. As he made his way back to his office he told himself sadly that Sir William's eldest son would be the ruin of his family.

After he had gone the baronet went to the breakfast room where Edward was just finishing a hearty breakfast, having been told by his servant that his father was engaged with the lawyer. He greeted him cheerfully and Sir William asked when he had arrived.

"About ten o'clock, sir. We came along at a fair pace."

"Did you see Vincent?"

"No, sir. I was told you were out and after I had dined I went straight to my bed."

"You do not know when Vincent came in?"

"He was not in at midnight, sir."

Sir William pulled the bell-rope and sent the servant to tell Mr. Vincent that he wished to see him in the library immediately, and the man returned with the information that Mr. Vincent had not returned home until past seven o'clock that morning and left word with his man that he was not to be disturbed until noon.

"He will be roused now," said Sir William shortly. "Tell his man to wake him and give him my message."

The servant vanished and Sir William asked Edward to attend him in the library until his brother came down. The library was a large if somewhat austere room, its shelves filled with books bound in leather with gold-embossed spines and the top shelf adorned with busts of Roman emperors. When the door had closed behind them the baronet told his son to sit down, lowering himself heavily into a wing chair beside the library table.

"Brayford confirms what he told me before," he said grimly. "Vincent's extravagance has gone beyond all reason."

The news did not surprise Edward, but he waited with some apprehension for his father to continue.

"When your brother came of age four years ago," said Sir William, "I made over to him the fortune I had inherited with Edgecombe Manor from my mother's uncle. I did not include the manor house in the gift but I settled on him instead an income of twelve thousand pounds a year, thinking that such a sum should be sufficient. When he is in London this house is at his disposal and he is welcome to use any of my carriages, though I draw the line at the horses. He is too bad a driver for that. He is allowed to stable his own here, however, and there is accommodation for his servants. I could not see what else he could want; a separate establishment was only necessary if he were married. I am afraid I did not allow for his extravagant tastes. Last autumn I discovered that he was in debt to his tailor for a sum above one thousand pounds and to his cordwainer for five hundred, and that he had not paid his coach-builder for the new curricle he smashed up by running it into a ditch on the way to Newmarket. When I confronted him with these things he brushed them aside, saying that all his friends kept their tradesmen waiting a twelvemonth, and that 'on his honor' he had no more debts than those. From what Brayford told me this morning I doubt if your brother knows the meaning of the word honor. He has spent every penny of my great-uncle's fortune and his year's income is already gone, though we are only in March. What does he think he is going to do over the next nine months?"

"He will live on credit, I daresay, sir. A great many men do."

"Not a Chevening!" Sir William's stern face showed

what he thought of this suggestion. "It seems that he cannot avoid the gaming tables. I daresay he spent the whole of last night at White's adding to his debts, and it must stop. If he is too weak to resist temptation it must be put out of his reach."

"I do not see how you can do that, sir."

"I have warned him before, so that he knows what to expect. He will leave directly for Rome, making a leisurely way through Europe, and you are to accompany him. You will not return to England until this time next year and during the months you are away you will see that he does not visit a casino or a race course. Fortunately your old tutor, Mr. Hayley, is at liberty and I have decided to send him with you as courier. He will hold the purse and you will both apply to him for any moneys you require."

However much the thought of visiting Rome might delight Edward under other conditions, the idea of being employed there as bear-leader to his brother appalled him. "Will Vincent agree?" he asked.

"If he does not," said Sir William calmly, "I shall refuse to pay any more of his debts and he will face a debtor's prison."

"You are not serious, sir?"

"I have never been more serious in my life." The baronet got up and walked to the fireplace. He stood a moment staring down at the sea coal that was burning there, and then he raised his eyes to the white stone of the chimney breast where two hounds were carved standing over the body of a hare. Beneath them was the motto of the Chevenings, *I Hold To My Course.* "Vincent shall not hold to his course," he said more to himself than to his son, and then raising his voice he added sarcastically,

"Perhaps you will oblige me by visiting your brother's room and finding out when he intends to do me the honor of waiting on me here."

His bitterness remained with Edward as he went to find Vincent, who was sitting up in bed drinking brandy and not making the slightest attempt to get up. "What the devil is the old man about, wanting to get me out of bed at this hour," he demanded when he saw his brother. "My head is splitting." Sir William's heir put down his empty glass and took his head in his hands as if he were afraid it might drop from his shoulders. "Did he say what he wanted?"

"Brayford has been with him," Edward said and saw his head come up sharply.

"Good God, that has sunk me!" said Vincent gloomily. "I conclude that our revered parent is acting the Roman father again?"

"He is not acting," said Edward. "And he is more Roman than I have ever seen him. I would advise you to get your man to work on you as speedily as possible."

Vincent studied his brother sourly. "And I would advise you to dismiss that man of yours," he said. "Your cravat is a disgrace, and as for the fit of that coat!" He shuddered. "Where did you have it made?"

"In Bath."

"It looks like it. I have seldom seen one worse cut. Pray take it and yourself off, my dear fellow."

Edward departed, leaving Vincent's valet to do his best with his master, obstructed from time to time by groans punctuated by oaths from Mr. Chevening. Half an hour later, Vincent presented himself in the library, pale but strengthened by the brandy and exquisitely dressed. The points of his starched collar touched his cheekbones, his snowy cravat was tied with care above his ruffled shirt, his new bottle-green coat sat on his shoulders without a wrinkle and his light trousers were strapped under the instep without a crease. "You wished to see me, sir?" he said mildly.

"I do. I sent for Brayford a little while ago because certain rumors had reached me about your affairs and I wished him to discover if they were true."

Vincent's handsome face took on an amused expression. "Do I understand, sir, that you set Brayford to spy on me?" he asked. "The poor little man must be exhausted—"

"Be silent, sir!" thundered his father, losing his patience and his temper. "If he had assured me this morning that there was no cause for alarm the matter would have ended there. But he tells me that you have dissipated your fortune in four years and your year's income in three months, and I am not being ruined, and the rest of your family beggared, because you cannot keep away from the gaming tables. I have told Edward what I intend for you and I shall now tell you."

When a somewhat chastened Vincent joined his brother later Edward asked him what their father had said.

"Oh, that I am to leave England at the end of next week," said Vincent airily. "Which will suit me very well, because the duns are after me more than he knows."

"He told me he would settle no more of your debts," Edward said and saw him smile.

"He said the same thing to me, threatening me with a debtor's prison. He did not like it by half when I said I'd always heard that the Marshalsea could be a very pleasant place given sufficient friends to visit one and servants to see to one's wants."

"Vin, you are incorrigible."

"I understand that he has arranged for you to accompany me," went on Vincent calmly, "which is an excellent plan, as I shall be able to tell my mother that I am taking you to Rome to indulge your pleasure in the great collections there. My nobility will be the theme of every conversation at Edgecombe for weeks to come." He laughed at Edward's expression. "I find myself in need of fresh air. I shall order my curricle and I will drive you down to Richmond and back."

"Thank you," said Edward, "But you may go alone. I do not care for the way you treat your horses and I have no wish to be killed."

After Vincent had gone Edward wrote a short letter to Frank Crayne, sending it round to his rooms in Manchester Street. In it he told him that he was leaving England with Vincent for Rome immediately, and he asked him to tender his deep regrets to Lucinda for having to miss her ball.

When Frank showed the letter to his sister she put her pretty head in the air and said she had no patience with Edward Chevening.

"I suppose Vincent Chevening is going abroad because of his debts," she said. "But I see no reason why his brother should accompany him."

"I do not suppose he had any choice in the matter."

"You mean that Sir William is sending him with Vincent? But why?"

"To cure his habit of gambling perhaps."

"But can anyone suppose that Edward Chevening is able to control his elder brother?"

Frank did not reply for a moment and then he said quietly, "I see that you share the opinion most people hold about Edward—that he is a gentle, self-effacing man who can be duped by anyone who puts a mind to it. You are mistaken, my dear. There are times when Edward can be extremely determined and will not hesitate to enforce his will on others if he thinks it right. It is a side to his nature that his family at Edgecombe have never seen. Sir William knew what he was about when he picked him to go with Vincent, and in my opinion it is the poor old gentleman's last desperate effort to save his heir from himself."

Frank was right when he said that there were sides to Edward that his family did not understand. Lady Chevening made no secret of the fact that Vincent was her favorite: with his fair good looks and high spirits and his charm of manner that made it easy for him to pass on to another any irksome duty that he did not wish to perform himself, who could resist him? But from a child Edward had nettled his mother with his independence, although she had tried to understand when he went his way quietly, asking nobody's permission for his harmless pursuits. Essentially fairminded, she had done her best to show him the same affection she had for his two brothers, knowing that she did not quite succeed.

Jasper was like Vincent in looks, and from the time he was twelve years old and had seen the mails decorated with laurel leaves coming down the Bath road with the news of the victory at Waterloo, the army was to be his career. In this ambition his fond mamma encouraged him, being certain that he was destined to be a second Wellington. She could not see that Edward was destined for anything. The only sport that he enjoyed was that of fisticuffs, where he was an apt pupil of old ex-champion Tod, who kept the Green Man in Edgecombe village.

As a lad Sir William had been trained in the science of milling by Gentleman Humphries in his rooms in Panton Street, where he had for his pupils most of the young sprigs of the nobility. The baronet had been delighted to discover that Champion Tod had retired from the ring at a time when his own sons were of an age to learn, and moreover that he was willing to combine his duties as landlord of the Green Man with private lessons to the sons of the local gentry.

The ex-champion's son, Benjamin, was large and brawny and although his father had set his face against him following him into the ring, he had no objection to his being brought in as a sparring partner to his paying pupils. When Benjamin became under-coachman at Edgecombe he was sometimes invited by Edward to a sparring match in the stable yard, the baronet's second son being somewhat of a perfectionist. One day the under-coachman told him that he did not think he could be faulted.

"Only one thing I'd like to mention, Mr. Edward," he added. "You did ought to put more force into your punches."

Edward said that he did not wish to send one of his father's coachmen to his duties with a blackened eye.

"You leave it to me to defend meself, Mr. Edward," said young Tod. "Just you put a bit o' strength be'ind it and try agin."

Edward tried again, with a punch to Benjamin's chest that floored him. "I'm extremely sorry, my dear fellow," he said as he helped him to his feet. "But you did tell me to try more strength behind my punches."

"I take back all I said, Mr. Edward," gasped young Tod, winded from his encounter with Edward's fist. "You could go into the ring professional any day you chose and I'd back you agin the 'eaviest man there, and I take my oath my father'd say the same."

Edward thanked him but after that he kept his heaviest punches for a leather bag stuffed with straw in an empty coach-house.

Sir William raised no objection when Edward asked if he might take the under-coachman abroad with him as his personal servant. He was off to Chevening that day and he would not see his son again before he left with Vincent for Paris, where they were to make their first stay, visiting Mme. St. Clair, a distant cousin of their mother's.

"Now remember," Sir William said as the traveling coach came round into the Square to take him into Kent, "I am trusting you to keep your brother away from the tables."

"I will do my best, sir," Edward said. "But I would bring to your notice that as I am three years younger than he is he may very well tell me to go to hell."

"I am aware of that, but I do not think it likely that he will knock you down."

"No, sir." Edward's rare smile showed itself for a moment. "I do not think he will do that." He added that it might be less difficult to persuade Vincent when the Channel was between him and some of his rich friends.

"You mean Mr. Delamere, I conclude? But he has a hundred thousand pounds a year in his own right. Vincent cannot attempt to equal men like Rick Delamere!"

"Perhaps when he is free of Delamere's company his tastes will moderate a little," said Edward, and then with a last handshake Sir William was off.

Lady Chevening received Vincent's explanation for the

trip to Rome thoughtfully. It was unlike him to put himself out in order to indulge Edward in the study of collections, in which he acknowledged he had no interest, and she wondered what lay behind it. It was Liz, though, who was most grieved to see Edward go.

"I shall miss you dreadfully," she wept as he lifted the heavy "Voyages" down for her for the last time. "And there is the Coronation in July and the fête in Green Park. You will miss it all."

"Funny little old-fashioned creature!" He tweaked her hair gently. "Mamma says I am turning you into a blue-stocking."

She brightened considerably when he gave her an address in Rome to which she could write to tell him about the Coronation, and she dried her eyes and watched him go with the "Voyages" left unopened on the library table.

The young Chevenings were given a warm welcome by Mme. St. Clair in Paris and stayed in her house a month, meeting a number of fashionable people who amused Vincent more than they did his brother. Monsieur St. Clair seldom visited Paris, being occupied with his estate near Lyons. The château had been looted by the revolutionaries more than twenty years before, but he was fortunate in that the house itself had not been destroyed, and he was doing his best to restore it as well as the estate, living in a few rooms of the château with only an old housekeeper to wait on him. When the two young Englishmen visited him there he was eager to learn all they could tell him about English husbandry. Edward did what he could to help him, but Vincent was too bored to stay longer than a week.

"I did not come all this way to be hectored about farming," he told his brother. "We have all we want of that sort of thing at Chevening. For God's sake let us go on to somewhere more interesting."

He chose Baden-Baden for their next visit and Edward reluctantly consented, hoping that the beauty of the Black Forest and the interesting old town might be sufficient to keep him from the gaming tables for which it was famous.

After their long and arduous journey over bad roads, he and Hayley did their best to keep Vincent from slipping away, but they were not entirely successful. The night before they were to leave for Italy Vincent told Edward he did not need him or Hayley with him that night, that he was no child needing a nursemaid, and he intended to see if his luck had changed.

"Not unless I come with you," Edward said, barring the way.

"Damn you, do you think you can stop me?" demanded Vincent angrily.

"I am afraid I may have to," Edward said apologetically.

"Stand out of my way if you don't wish to be knocked down," said Vincent, and as Edward did not budge he rushed at him with such purpose that Edward was forced to deliver one of the punches that Tod had so much admired, with the same result. He stood back, waiting for his elder brother to get his breath back, and when he did, instead of cursing him, to Edward's surprise he laughed. Scrambling to his feet he declared with amazement that he did not know Edward had it in him. "Took me in completely," he said good-humoredly. "Very well, we will visit the tables together, as long as we can leave that damned old woman Hayley behind."

He did not lose a great deal that night, and from that day his respect for his younger brother grew. He even apologized for being a drag on him. "I know you dislike this sort of thing," he told him. "You would much rather spend your time looking at picture galleries and art collections, but when we reach Italy I promise you will be free to do what you like."

They had a hair-raising journey over the Alps. Edward was entranced by the long ranges of mountains rising snow-capped against deep blue skies, although the passes were so narrow that more than once they had to get out and walk in case the carriage went over into a precipice. On one occasion they had to wait for hours while Tod and Vincent's man, helped by a local waggoner, dug it out of a ditch.

They went first to Florence, where it was airless and too warm for comfort, and from there they made their way to Naples, where it rained steadily for a fortnight. They were glad to reach Rome at last and the rooms in a spacious palazzo that had been hired for them by Lord Dunfoyne, an old friend of Sir William's who had been residing in the city for the best part of five years.

In a very short while, with the aid of the hospitable Irish baron, they acquired a circle of English acquaintances, some amusing and some whom Vincent declared to be bores. A round of entertainment followed, under scorching Italian skies.

Vincent found the Italian young ladies entrancing to look at, but the decorum that hedged them round insupportable.

"One cannot talk to a girl without her duenna listening

to every word," he complained to his brother. "Once when I asked that delightful Isabella—whose surname I forget—to send her lady away she was shocked. In Italy it would not be considered at all proper. I do not see why I, an Englishman, should be judged according to the depraved behavior of Italian gentlemen."

His disgust with the duennas of Rome led him to consent to accompany Edward to Padua, and then on to Venice, where Edward would have liked to linger awhile. He was able, however, to persuade his brother to visit the Lido, where Lord Byron was accustomed to ride by the shores of the Adriatic.

Fortunately they arrived back in Rome at the time that Clara Dunfoyne came out from England to join her father, and Vincent turned his back happily on the prudish Italians and devoted his time and attentions to Clara, who was young, pretty, and a chatterer. For the rest of the winter he was assiduous in his attendance on her and appeared to be so much under the spell of her bright eyes that Edward felt free to enjoy some of the museums and art galleries and the private collections of Englishmen who had settled abroad.

Vincent laughed about his brother's tastes. "I knew when Edward came back to Rome he would bring his Oxford ways with him," he said to Hayley. "To me they are nothing but a dead bore."

"Perhaps Mr. Edward is making the most of his opportunities," the old tutor said. "He may not have so many chances as you will to see such things again, so that it cannot matter to you if you do not take advantage of them now."

"You are perfectly right." Vincent had the grace to look a trifle ashamed. "We all trade on Edward's good nature too much, and I know my father keeps him damnably short of money. He has not the quarter of what I have, and yet he seems able to buy his pictures and so on without a great deal of trouble. I do not suppose he has ever been in debt in his life." And he went off to spend a few more English pounds on a charming toy— a clockwork bird in a gilded cage—to amuse the pretty Clara.

Edward encouraged the affair, hoping it might end in an engagement, and he was taken aback when his brother told him at the end of February that he was cutting short his stay and returning to England.

"The truth is," he said with a look of half-comical dismay on his handsome face, "I have got to get married."

"Clara Dunfoyne—" began Edward eagerly.

"Oh no." Vincent laughed. "Charming as she is, the Dunfoynes have no money, and that is no use to me. It is Sarah Wakefield who must rescue me from my difficulties."

"What do you mean?" Edward did not like to think of what was in his mind.

"I mean I shall have to marry her," said Vincent impatiently. "I know she is damned ugly but she inherits a fortune of one hundred thousand pounds when she marries, and before she and Maria have their coming-out ball this season I mean to make sure of her. She has always been devoted to me, and my engagement to the Wakefield heiress ought to quieten some of the gentlemen who were clamoring for their money before I left England."

Edward remembered his father's anger upon discovering Vincent's debts and wondered what other shocks had been in store for him after they left. "You mean you were in debt when we started out?" he said.

"As heavily as I could be. Brayford did not know the half of it." Vincent laughed and clapped his brother on the shoulder. "I have no doubt my father has settled everything for me by this time, and that is why we have had no word from him since we've been gone. Our Roman parent was in no mood to write to his profligate son. But he will forgive me when I announce my engagement to Sarah, and all the tradesmen will be back, begging for my patronage and offering credit as long as your arm. My dear fellow, do not look down that long nose of yours. If you were to find yourself a rich wife you would have far more to spend on the trifles you hanker after, and as the second son of our family you have not a great fortune to anticipate."

Edward did not think that Vincent would have one either if he returned to his previous habits when he reached England. He saw him off with the faithful Hayley on the following day, and although he was now free to indulge in his own pleasure, he found that the delight of the Rome visit had gone. Looking at pictures of which until then he had only seen poor copies, and taking in his hand illuminated manuscripts or books of hours—the illustrations in colors and gold so brilliant that it seemed they must have been executed yesterday—had lost their appeal, and even while he admired them, there was the nagging worry of Vincent at the back of his mind.

And then he received a belated letter from Frank Crayne that had been posted months ago and followed him around Europe. It contained a half-humorous account of his sister's successes. She was indeed, he said, a young lady of fashion these days. If sleeves were to be full, hers were balloons; if bonnets were to be in the French style, hers came direct from Paris; and when white kid boots were the rage she wore only yellow or pink. "The men are round her like bees," Frank concluded, "and she will have none of them. Uncle Herbert has returned to Crayne to nurse an attack of gout."

Edward felt it was time that he followed his brother home.

Four

    It had astonished and overawed Sarah when Vincent sought her out at Edgecombe to be the object of his attentions. His pursuit of her was brief but highly gratifying; too many of Maria's friends had in the past pitied her for her looks, her mousy-colored hair and short, sturdy stature. She would have given worlds to possess the tall elegance of Maria and the loveliness of Lucinda Crayne. The envy of the local young ladies was very pleasant in consequence, and she was flattered out of her seventeen-year-old wits by Vincent's preference. It had not occurred to her that the heir to the Chevening title and estates would seriously consider her for his wife, and when he asked her to marry him it took her only a moment to accept. Had he not been her hero since she came to Chevening when she was eight years old?

Lady Chevening told her husband that she was delighted. "I can admit now, William," she said, "that I was dreading a London season with an heiress on my hands. Sarah is such an unsophisticated little creature; she might easily have become the prey of some unscrupulous fortune-hunter. Whereas nobody can accuse Vincent of that! He has a fortune of his own, besides being heir to Chevening."

Sir William was not so happy about it. The morning after Edward returned to find his family installed in St. James's Square, with Vincent playing the part of an attentive lover to a deliriously happy Sarah, his father took him into the library to inquire after his friends in Rome and to speak his mind about the engagement.

"I wish with all my heart that I had never offered Sarah a home with us," he said. "I should have packed her off to her own people, the Wakefields of Corrieford. They were her rightful guardians, and then this engagement would never have come about."

"But she appears to be extremely happy, sir."

"She may be, poor child, but Vincent is only after her money and you know it as well as I do." He broke off with a frown of displeasure, and then continued abruptly: "After you left his bills came in like snowflakes; he owed hundreds of pounds to every tradesman in London. I have paid them all now, but it has not been easy, with the entertaining your mother is planning for this great coming-out ball at Easter and the wedding at Chevening later on. I have told her nothing of it, of course—I do not want to spoil her pleasure."

"Do you not think, sir, that marriage with a practical little body like Sarah may give Vincent the sense of responsibility that he needs?"

"I can but hope that it will." Sir William tried to dismiss it from his mind. "I see that you have brought home several packing cases full of treasures to add to your collection." He smiled tolerantly. "Someday you must tell me what there is in it—I have not time now. I am expecting Brayford at any moment. He is preparing the draft of the marriage settlement to be sent to Adams, the Wakefields' man of business in Corrieford, for his approval and suggestions." He got up and laid his hand with an affectionate pressure on his son's shoulder. "It is good to have you home, Edward. I feel that I have at least one member of my family on whom I can depend."

The Chevening ball was a brilliant start to the London season. The huge ballroom was redolent with the scent of flowers that filled the two great fireplaces and massed in every corner, and the long pier glasses mirrored the light from scores of candles, adding to the brilliance of the great chandeliers.

Edward, gallantly doing his duty in the shadow of his more popular brothers, looked for one person in vain, until suddenly he found himself next to her at the end of a dance.

As his eyes met Lucinda's he knew he had found the reason for his return home.

"Miss Crayne," he said, bowing. "Your servant, ma'am!"

"Mr. Chevening!" She dropped him a curtsy, her dark eyes mocking him. "So you are home at last. I hope you intend to ask me to dance, because I would remind you, sir, that you have kept me waiting for a year."

"I would ask you for the next dozen dances," he told her with a smile, "if I were not sure that I would make an enemy of every other man in the room." His eyes dwelt on her with a gratifying admiration: her high-waisted dress of yellow taffeta, with a green sash that matched the Crayne emeralds glowing in her hair and at her throat, made her look far lovelier than he had remembered her. "I broke my side of our bargain through no choice of my own," he said.

"Oh, did we make a bargain?" Affectation suddenly crept into her manner. "I was not aware of it. I thought we were interrupted before you could conclude a lecture that I scarcely considered necessary." She saw his expression stiffen, and was angry with herself for attacking him, yet because of what she had recently heard of him and of others of his family she felt impelled to continue. "But perhaps you may find me wiser than I was then!"

"That I shall hope to discover." He had withdrawn into his old cool self, and as the music began he held out his hand to her. "Shall we dance?"

She let him lead her onto the floor and he was immediately aware of the glances of the other men. She was, no doubt of it, one of the most sought-after girls in the room. But at Edgecombe he had asked her not to change and she had changed: the world she was moving in now had touched her with its easy flattery and hypocrisy. The innocent charm of the girl whose earring he had mended at Edgecombe was gone, and a bleakness of spirit descended upon him.

"How long are you to be in London?" he asked as if he were asking the question of any girl there, having little interest in the answer.

"My Aunt Winter is giving me a second season in Manchester Square." She was extremely self-possessed but her eyes were provocative. "I thought you said you did not dance? I can find no fault with your performance tonight."

"You forget I have been under Vincent's tutelage for the past year."

"Ah yes—Vincent." She glanced across the room to where Vincent was dancing with Sarah. "What a charming man he is—so popular with everyone. Such a fund of conversation and wit!"

The sarcasm in her voice made him defend his brother. "I am sorry he has incurred your displeasure," he said.

"Incurred my displeasure? What can you mean? I find him excessively diverting. 'Lucinda,' he said to me not a fortnight ago, 'have you no rich uncles or aunts or perhaps a wealthy grandfather to leave you a fortune?' 'My dear Vincent,' I said—because we are on very good terms, Frank being such an old friend of the family—'my dear Vincent, all my relatives with large fortunes have large families to match, and those relatives who have no families have no money either!' "

Her laugh made Rick Delamere, who was dancing next to them, turn his head. "Miss Crayne," he said, "you gave my dance to Edward. I shall claim two more instead."

"You shall have them," she told him, and catching the look she gave that dissolute young man, Edward wondered why he had not stayed in Rome.

He did not speak to her again until he happened to look into the small drawing-room in search of a lady his mother had sent him to find. Four dowagers were gossiping in one corner, their plumed headdresses nodding, but his mother's friend was not with them, and he was turning away when he saw Miss Crayne standing by the open windows looking down at the Square. She was sipping a glass of iced negus with a thoughtful expression on her face. He hesitated, not knowing whether to speak to her, when she turned her head and saw him.

"You find London different from Rome, I conclude," she said a marked coolness.

"There are many treasures to be seen there," he replied with equal detachment.

"Oh, I was not thinking of works of art." She gave a small shrug. "You need not pretend with me, Mr. Chevening. We have all heard of the young lady who at last persuaded you to take your nose out of books and yourself out of picture galleries. Clara's letters to her brother, Gerald Dunfoyne, have been full of the fascinating Mr. Chevening. Your brother has kept us extremely amused with his account of how you lost your heart at last."

He frowned, angered by this attack upon himself and pretty little Clara. "I beg your pardon. I was not at first aware of what you were saying. Miss Clara Dunfoyne was in Rome when we were there; she is a most charming young lady. Everyone was delighted with her."

"Were they indeed? Then I hope I shall meet her when she comes to England. But I understand that she is not fashionable in her dress—in fact, her brother describes her as a fright!"

Edward flushed indignantly. "Mr. Gerald Dunfoyne does his sister an injustice. She dresses simply, I believe, but with excellent taste, and he should be proud of her. And there are other things in her favor—there is a simplicity about her and a charm of manner devoid of any affectation that others might do well to imitate."

Turning abruptly, he left the room. She stared after him angrily, feeling that she had had the worst of the encounter and was glad when Gerald Dunfoyne returned to release her from the whispering dowagers.

Edward avoided her for the rest of the night. She was always surrounded with admirers eager for her favors, and he was glad to oblige his mother by dancing with young ladies who had none.

As he danced, however, his anger against her faded and was directed toward another. Vincent had indeed staged a very neat revenge for the months when he had to endure his younger brother's surveillance. No doubt in her letters home Miss Dunfoyne had spoken of "Mr. Chevening" in glowing terms, not specifying which one, and if Edward told the truth he would not be believed and would hurt little Sarah and cast a shadow over her happiness.

That could not be done. His shoulders were broad enough to bear the teasing of his family and friends, until sooner or later Miss Dunfoyne came home to explain it for herself.

But Lucinda was a different matter altogether. In the midst of his sadness at finding her so changed, he hoped against hope that she had been behaving much as the schoolgirl at Crayne had behaved years ago to attract his attention and interest. He did not think it likely. The world he detested had caught her up in its toils and would not lightly let her go.

As he traveled home with Tod and his packing cases it had occurred to him that he might find a house of his own in London in which to house his modest collection and where he could entertain his friends, and after that night he determined to do so without delay.

The following day he set out in search of what he wanted and discovered a dwelling in Sloane Street that was admirably suited to his purposes.

During the days of the Regency several schools for

young ladies and gentlemen had prospered in the district, the patrons being French emigrés, but after these people had returned to France taking their teachers with them, the schools had moved away to more salubrious districts. Sloane Street was now slightly down-at-heel and much given to lodging-houses, but the landlord of the house to which Edward took a fancy was asking a low rent and there was a large room on the first floor that would make a good gallery. He arranged to move in at the end of the following week, and forgot completely that Sloane Street was near the barracks where his brother Jasper had his lodging.

That evening as they sat alone for once at dinner, the rest of the family being at a concert, he told his father what he had done.

Sir William was inclined to be skeptical. "You say you have taken this house for your collection, inspired no doubt by those you saw in Rome," he said. "But my dear Edward, those collections are owned by wealthy men who think nothing of spending thousands of pounds on one picture. Do you intend to emulate them?"

"No, sir. My collection will be valued by nobody but myself. I intend to include in it unconsidered pictures and trifles that have little general appeal or monetary worth."

"But why do you select Sloane Street? It is not a particularly pleasant or fashionable neighborhood."

"That is why the house is not dear. There are ten good rooms, all high-pitched and wainscoted, four attic rooms for servants' bedrooms, with fireplaces, and plenty of space below the house for a servants' hall and kitchen quarters and men-servants' lodgings. There is a garden too, and good stabling, and the whole costs no more than twenty pounds a year."

"I see you have gone into the matter in some depth, but will you not need a larger income to pay for a separate establishment?"

"Certainly not, sir. My income is ample for my needs and I have no liabilities."

His mother thought it tiresome of Edward to decide to move to a house of his own in the middle of the London season. "He takes himself off just when I had been depending on him as an escort for his sisters," she told her husband.

"Vincent will be here, my dear," said Sir William.

"But his attention will all be for Sarah!"

"Well then, there is Jasper. I know he is a fool, but he is always ready to be the girls' companion at any social function in London. He dances almost better than he sits a horse."

"You are not to call our youngest son a fool, William!" Sophia Chevening tried to be indignant and then she laughed. "Well, perhaps he has not the brains of Edward or such a knowledge of the world as Vincent." She returned to the vexed question of Edward's house. "It means that every time I need him I shall have to send a note to Sloane Street," she complained. "And he is so useful at talking to old ladies who fancy themselves neglected, and in dancing with wallflowers at a ball where girls outnumber the men."

When Edward asked his mother if she could spare the time to come and see his house she replied crisply that he could ask her again at the end of the summer when the wedding was over. It was to be at Chevening, with all the grandeur of oxen roasted in the park and a tenants' ball like the one that had characterized Vincent's coming-of-age, and she said she would have to leave London at the end of July to discuss the lists of houseguests with the housekeeper there.

"In the meantime you are not going to escape me," she warned her second son. "I am depending on your help at all my parties and you will ignore my notes at your peril."

"They shall have my immediate attention," he promised her and returned to his house with the feeling that his newfound freedom would be broken into with some frequency during the summer months.

Certainly as the London Season went on its way his sister and Sarah appeared to be engaged to the full with balls, concerts, plays, dinners and parties every night. They were presented to His Majesty, who gave two fingers to Sarah and kissed Maria on the cheek, and Edward, hearing of all this dissipation, came to the conclusion that the female stamina for all its appearance of fragility was infinitely stouter than that of the male.

One day in May, after he had unpacked the last of his cases and had finished arranging its contents on the shelves in the gallery of his new house, he went for a walk in the park. His eye was caught by a lady's phaeton, a delightful little carriage drawn by two ponies. Such carriages were extremely popular that summer, the king having set the fashion by having one to drive himself round Windsor Great Park, and Edward was admiring the little turn-out when suddenly it stopped and he was summoned to it with an imperious wave of a hand.

The groom dismounted to hold the ponies' heads and Edward went to the carriage to be greeted by Lady Winter and her niece.

After Lady Winter had expressed her pleasure at seeing him again, saying that there had been time only for the merest formalities at his sister's ball, Lucinda asked him if it were true that he now had his own house in London.

He admitted that it was, and when he told her where it was situated she did not turn up her nose at Sloane Street but remarked that the school she had attended in Highgate had started life there, and it had had the reputation then for being a quiet neighborhood.

"Sloane Street is still quiet enough for my taste," he told her, and saw her smile.

"But you were always a man of sober tastes," she reminded him. It was almost as if she were asking him to be friends again, and although she was extremely elegant in her pale blue pelisse and white crepe bonnet with a wreath of cornflowers round its crown, for just a moment she was the girl he had known at Edgecombe, and the May morning was the brighter for it.

"My husband is suffering from an acute attack of gout," said Lady Winter, glancing from his serious face to her niece's subdued one with interest. "But directly he is over it I shall send him to call on you, Mr. Chevening. We have heard much about your collection from Frank."

He said that he was afraid Frank had the bias of a long friendship and that his few possessions would scarcely interest a connoisseur of Sir Berkeley's standing, but he would be honored to see him nevertheless. After a few more polite exchanges the ladies drove on.

"That young man is very taken with you, my dear," said her ladyship. "He could not take his eyes off you."

Lucinda laughed lightly. "My dearest aunt, if I were a picture or a piece of sculpture, or even a scrap of carved Chinese jade, he would love me dearly and not rest until he could add me to his collection. But as I am only a woman—and not a prude like Clara Dunfoyne—I cannot foresee him ever asking me to become a permanent resident in his house."

"He is a true Chevening," said Lady Winter, remembering the time when his father had been one of the most sought-after young men in London. "And I do not think Clara Dunfoyne is a prude." She added after a moment, "You danced four dances with Rick Delamere at the Chevening ball. He is *not* a desirable young man, Lucinda, although he may be one of the richest."

"He is quite insufferable," agreed her niece. "He had the impertinence to allude to my Uncle Herbert as 'that old skinflint at Crayne.' I said, 'Mr. Delamere, however much I may abuse my uncle myself, I do not allow others to abuse him in my hearing. My Uncle Herbert is a kind and generous man and Frank and I are extremely attached to him!' "

"I hope he apologized?"

"He did not. He only laughed and told me to sheath my claws."

"The wretch!" But Lady Winter laughed and presently she observed, "I have only one bone to pick with Lord Crayne. He has made you too particular where young men are concerned. He has taught you to look for perfection where none exists. You have had several extremely good offers, my dear."

Her uncle had indeed taught her to seek perfection, Lucinda thought, and although it surely did not exist in heartless young wretches like Vincent and his friend Delamere, she wondered if it might exist in the grave sobriety of Edward Chevening. She did not know how to be sure.

In the large room on the first floor of his new house by the light of the four long windows, Edward returned to his collection. He found that the memory of Lucinda's face framed in its charming bonnet had a habit of coming between him and the objects in his gallery. He kept hearing the tones of her voice, almost asking for his forbearance, and he thought he could find a resemblance between her gentler look that morning and the serenity of his little madonna.

"Edward my boy," he told himself ruefully, "if you do not take care you will be in considerable danger of falling in love with that worldly young woman."

A morning call from his father at that moment came as a welcome interruption to thoughts that he felt were getting beyond his control.

Sir William came to present him with a statue of Hermes that had adorned the entrance hall at Chevening, and was reputed to have been brought back from Rome by Nollekens and sold to the late Sir George Chevening as an antique.

"Your grandfather paid Nollekens nearly a thousand pounds for it," Sir William told his son. "And as time goes on no doubt it will increase in value." He looked about him at the pictures on the paneled walls and the objects that were waiting to find a place on the shelves.

Mr. Brayford had a young clerk by the name of Tom Grimble who was interested in attending auction sales, and on visiting the lawyer over the lease of his house Edward was pleased to discover the young man and to employ him in buying things that caught his fancy. The day before, Mr. Grimble had attended Mr. Christie's Great Rooms in Pall Mall to purchase for him the marble head of a faun, a white porcelain cock of the Ch'ing Dynasty, and a Canton China punch bowl decorated with an English fox hunt. The baronet stared at these new treasures for some moments before inquiring what Edward had paid for them.

Edward said that Grimble was astute and knew that he seldom paid more than ten pounds for a thing. "He gave two pounds for the faun, four for the white cock, and seven for the bowl."

"Extraordinary." As the servants who had accompanied Sir William staggered up the back stairs with the Hermes and deposited it in the middle of the room, the baronet waited for his son's appreciation of a considerably more valuable object. As always, though, Edward was restrained in his thanks. He told the man to remove the coverings and to stand the statue between two of the windows, and then he turned to his father and held out his hand.

"It is good of you to spare Hermes from his niche at Chevening, sir," he said. "And I shall treasure him—not because of his value—but because you gave him to me."

And with that the baronet had to be content. "A queer fellow, that second son of yours," he told Sophia later, having found her in her sitting room in St. James's Square making out a list of guests for her next dinner party. "He does not seem fully to appreciate the Hermes. He was far more taken up with a collection of rubbishy objects on his shelves to which he added three more this morning. There was a good picture over the chimney-piece, though. He took Grimble down to Stanmore where there was a sale at a big house outside the village, and he instructed him to buy a basket containing some old books and a rolled-up canvas that had been cut from its frame in a chimney-piece similar in size to his own. I must say it fits in there very well. He says it is by John

Constable, and I daresay he is right. It resembles one of his country scenes."

"Mr. Constable is always painting country scenes," said Lady Chevening. "One sees them everywhere. He has painted far too many." And she returned to the list of her guests.

Five

As the summer went on Vincent did not seem quite as happy as he had been in the first few weeks of his engagement, and one evening he dropped in to dinner with his brother in Sloane Street to tell him why. Remembering the stories he had spread about himself and Clara Dunfoyne, Edward did not receive him with any great degree of cordiality, but Vincent was too full of his own affairs to notice. After abusing the house and its district and asking querulously if the mutton his housekeeper provided was always as tough as the piece put before them that night, he spoke of Sarah's uncle, Samuel Wakefield.

"I wish I liked him better than I do," he said. "I know that when she marries me her fortune will pass into my control, but in the meantime he is being remarkably close-fisted over it."

Politely, but without revealing a great deal of interest, Edward asked what had happened.

"Nobody could think me unreasonable, I suppose," said his brother truculently, "in writing to the old ruffian suggesting that as I was to become Sarah's husband on the first of September it would not come amiss if he were to advance me some thousands of pounds on her account. I pointed out that I was incurring considerable expense in finding and furnishing a suitable house for her in London, and that I was also considering enlarging Wakefield House and adding several thousands of acres to the estate. I could not consent to live there as it stands; it is paltry and ordinary to a degree."

Edward remarked that he had always considered Wakefield House to be very comfortable.

Vincent dismissed his brother's opinion contemptuously. "I have no doubt that a small property might appeal to you, Edward, because, my dear fellow—meaning no offense—you and your friends have minds that are content with small and unimportant things. One has only to examine that so-called collection of yours upstairs to see that. But it will not do for me. My mind is turned to bigger properties than Wakefield!"

Disregarding his brother's opinion of his friends, his mind and his collection, Edward asked what Mr. Wakefield's reply had been.

"Why, the old devil wrote a stiff letter saying that only after the marriage settlement had been drawn up and signed would he consider parting with a penny of his niece's money, and that as my father was a rich man he suggested that I should apply to him to advance what was required. What do you think of that? Does he not sound like a tight-fisted old crib?"

"You do not think that he thought he was doing what was right for Sarah?"

"I do not think anything of the sort. If I read him aright he will not part with a fortune that size until the last moment. Why, he has not even asked me to visit him in Yorkshire to talk the matter over, or suggested meeting me as Sarah's future husband. His address, by the way, is a grand one—Corrieford Hall—and it may be that he does not wish me to discover how very well he is living there on Sarah's income."

"I am sure that cannot be so."

"And I am sure of nothing," Vincent said, "until that fortune is in my hands."

And Sarah's happiness too, thought Edward, as he watched his brother drive away later that night in the new curricle with its fine pair of matched bays that he had bought since his engagement to Sarah had been made public. He wondered if Vincent remembered Sarah as often as he remembered her fortune.

A date had been fixed at the end of July for Mr. Wakefield to come to London to meet Sir William and sign the marriage settlement. London was emptying fast, and in his inconsequent way Vincent had arranged to leave for the Delameres' place near Eldon in Surrey, eleven miles from London, directly the settlement had been signed, intending to stay there until a few days before the wedding. His friendship with Rick Delamere had resumed its old intimacy, a fact that Edward viewed with distrust and not a little apprehension.

On the day that Mr. Wakefield was to arrive, Lady Chevening had taken her two daughters to visit one of her sisters-in-law in London, while Vincent took Sarah out driving in his new curricle. It was a very superior article, and every head turned to look at the handsome driver and the beautiful pair of bays.

Sir William and Mr. Brayford waited in the library in St. James's Square for Mr. Wakefield, and when the appointed hour had come and gone a servant was dispatched to the hotel where he was to have stayed the night to discover if the gentleman had been taken ill. The man returned to say that Mr. Wakefield had not arrived at the hotel and that no letter had been furnished to account for his absence. Sir William concluded that he must have mistaken the day and that a letter of explanation and apology would herald his arrival at a later date. It was not until two days later, when Lady Stroud appeared with a letter from Corrieford, that they learned the reason for Mr. Wakefield's nonappearance.

Minnie Stroud, Sir William's favorite sister, had moved into Chevening Place with her husband to be with old Lady Chevening after Sir George's death, and when the old lady died they stayed on. Sir Henry Stroud had died of apoplexy in the New Year and Minnie, now alone, found that decisions in an emergency such as the present one left her quite unprepared.

"I suppose I should have sent it by a servant," she said, embracing her brother. "But as it was an express from Corrieford I fancied that Mr. Wakefield must have thought you intended him to come to Chevening for your meeting."

"But I have a letter in his own hand to say that he would meet me here in St. James's Square on the morning of the twenty-fourth of July and it is two days past that now." Sir William frowned at the letter in his hand. "This is not in his writing. It is from his lawyer, Adams."

"Then he must have been taken ill," said Lady Stroud with relief. "That explains it all."

The letter certainly explained why Mr. Wakefield had not kept his appointment with Sir William on the twenty-fourth of July; the gentleman had blown his brains out on the twenty-third. His man of business added that he would be obliged if Sir William could come to Corrieford in person as he urgently wished to discuss Miss Sarah's affairs with him.

"I will set out today." Sir William kissed his sister and sent for the housekeeper to arrange rooms for her and her maid and to provide refreshments after her journey.

"Oh, Will, I do trust that poor little Sarah's fortune is safe." Lady Stroud was almost in tears. "I felt it to be bad news—I had a premonition directly it arrived, which is why I came along so fast. Is Sarah here?"

"She is out driving with Vincent, and Sophia has taken the girls to call on your sister Miranda. Do not worry unduly, Minnie, my dear. On the only occasion that I met Mr. Wakefield, after Bella's funeral, he struck me as being a man of integrity. But there is the marriage settlement to be arranged and signed and he must have appointed somebody to be Sarah's guardian in his place. It is no doubt with that person I shall have to deal in Corrieford. Brayford had better come with me."

The attorney was sent for and the traveling carriage ordered to be ready to take them north at once. Within the hour the baronet and the lawyer were off, leaving the family to hear the news from Lady Stroud when they returned.

Sarah showed no concern for her uncle's death; he was a stranger to her and she had not seen him since he came to Wakefield House after her stepmother's death. It was

Vincent to whom her eyes went directly she heard the news, and she saw the dismay he was unable to hide and knew that he was very concerned indeed. He made no effort to stop her when she said she would go to her room.

The two girls were sent after her, but she preferred to be alone. The thoughts that were uppermost in their minds, however, were also in everyone else's: Could anything have happened to Sarah's fortune, and had Mr. Wakefield killed himself rather than give an account of where it had gone?

While they waited for news Lady Chevening went on quietly with her preparations for the wedding and told Lady Stroud that she must stay with them until after the ceremony on the first of September. "It is sad that Sarah should have lost her uncle under such circumstances," she said. "But as he was virtually a stranger to the child there can be no reason for postponing the wedding, although it must be held quietly in London, of course, and not, as we had planned, at Chevening."

Vincent was not so easily reassured. He rode out by himself and took to spending his evenings in the company of his friend Delamere. His mounting fears were only too soon realized.

When Sir William returned he called Sarah and Vincent into the library and told them briefly that Samuel Wakefield had spent every penny of his niece's fortune. With the exception of her mother's jewelry, which was of no great value, and the house in Kent, Sarah had nothing.

"The only excuse I can find for Mr. Wakefield is that times have been very bad in the north," said Sir William heavily, as the two young people stood silent before him. "He used the money to keep his mills going and his hands employed, otherwise it would have meant starvation for many and ruin for himself."

"But he was still ruined," said Vincent contemptuously. "And he has dragged Sarah down with him. Not a pretty situation, sir."

"It is my fault as much as his. When Sarah became part of my family, I should have made it my business to visit Corrieford from time to time, or sent Brayford to look into her affairs. But I trusted the man, and she was not my relative in fact, though I have looked on her for a long time as another daughter—as you soon will be, my dear," added the baronet with a smile at her.

He waited for his son to make a comment and then went on with some impatience, "Come, Vincent, don't stand there scowling and silent. It is distressing but it is not the end of the world. You will have to start your married life on a less lavish scale than you had planned and give up all thought of a London house of your own, but there are rooms in plenty here that are never used. Select those you like best for your own use and I will have them decorated and furnished to your taste. And there is Wakefield House; Brayford has given Sarah's tenants notice to leave as you wished him to do, and it will be your country home."

"But I cannot live there as it is now," protested Vincent. "I have planned extensive rebuilding—"

"Then it must wait," said his father sharply.

"And Wakefield House has only one hundred acres," went on Vincent. "How can I invite my friends to shoot over a hundred acres? I should be the laughingstock of London."

"There is always Chevening open to your friends when they arrive with their guns and their powder horns," said

Sir William mildly. "I can see no insurmountable difficulty there." He added after a moment, "In fact, I see
no reason why you should not entertain your friends at
Chevening Place if Wakefield House is not grand enough
for them. It is large enough in all conscience, and there
is plenty of game on its preserves."

Sophia was equally reconciled to Sarah's loss of fortune,
and she told Vincent with unusual tartness that she did
not know why he was making such a pother of it.

"You have plenty of money," she reminded him.
"Twelve thousand pounds a year besides the fortune your
father settled on you when you came of age. That should
be enough for a young couple to keep house on very comfortably. From the business you are making of it one
might imagine you had nothing of your own and were
dependent on Sarah's fortune alone!"

Vincent flung out in a huff. "I am afraid," Sophia said
with a rather stiff little smile at Minnie Stroud who had
been a witness of the scene, "I spoiled my dearest Vincent
when he was a child and he has repaid me by growing
into an equally spoiled young man."

The following morning, her eldest son took his be-
trothed out for a drive in his smart curricle and told her
that he had been thinking about their engagement all
night and had come to the conclusion that he must release
her from it. Sarah laughed and tucked her hand into his
arm.

"My darling Vincent," she said, "we shall not be
exactly poverty-stricken, I hope! If you do not wish to
live in St. James's Square there must be plenty of more
modest dwellings where we could settle down very comfortably, and I daresay you will be able to extend Wakefield House as you had planned after all. As long as we

love each other nothing else matters, and though we may not be able to live on the grand scale you had planned for me, you must know by this time that I am not at all a grand person, and as long as I am your wife I shall be utterly content."

Vincent said no more, but he lashed at the bays savagely, and glancing at his handsome face, Sarah caught a look of anger in it that frightened her a little. It was a moment she was to remember in the months ahead.

Six

In the meantime, Jasper, who had fallen into the habit of calling on Edward on his way to and from the barracks, told him that in his opinion Vincent was taking the loss of Sarah's fortune far more calmly than he had expected.

"Not that I have discussed it with him, mark you," he added. "But as he is going to Eldon to stay with Rick until the wedding it seems as if it is a blow from which he has recovered." They exchanged smiles. "Those bays of his are magnificent specimens," went on Jasper enviously. "Wish I had mounts like 'em."

"And Sarah?" asked Edward. "What are her feelings?"

"Oh, she is perfectly happy with the arrangements my father has made for them."

"I am glad of that." It was just possible, Edward supposed, that Vincent had discovered a real affection for his little Yorkshire lass and would try to mend his ways.

In the meantime Vincent had joined the house party in Surrey and spent his time riding, driving out in his new curricle, and making absurd wagers. Old Delamere allowed his son and his friends to behave as they liked; he kept to his room and joined them at dinner. He had separated from his wife some years previously and Lady Harriet Delamere now lived in Brighton, where she had a house on the Steine. Both parents indulged their only son to the greatest possible extent.

In Vincent's absence the good-natured Jasper, assisted by other young officers in his regiment, formed his sister's and Sarah's escort, very smart in their shakos, their frogged jackets, and with their spurs jingling on the boots under their light trousers. They were not, however, the only ones to put themselves out for the young ladies' entertainment.

One morning Lucinda arrived in St. James's Square in her aunt's barouche, which had been placed at her disposal for the day, and she invited the three girls to accompany her and to select a place they would like to visit.

A drive in the country was fixed upon, and the Star and Garter Hotel in Richmond was the spot chosen for luncheon. "And on the way," Lucinda said, "I intend to call on your brother Edward. My aunt promised that my uncle should call upon him when he recovered from the gout, but he has gone to Bath to take the waters and we are to follow him there next week. I am entrusted with their apologies."

Edward's house had been freshly painted and there was a brass knocker in the shape of a lion's head on the front door, shining like gold in the sunshine. Tod said that his master was at home and would be pleased to see them.

In the gallery upstairs Edward was in his shirtsleeves and received his sisters and Sarah with affection and their fashionable friend with more ceremony, apologizing for his dress. "I have been hanging some new pictures," he explained, his eyes on Miss Crayne, whose pale pink dress and small hat with its crown composed entirely of flowers made her look like a flower herself on that fine summer's day.

"Where is the Hermes?" asked Maria, looking about her, and when he pointed it out to her in its place between the windows, she said in her mother's sharp way that it should stand in the middle of the room.

"Well, I daresay it will stand there later on," he replied equably, and drew her attention to a case of newly acquired cameos in amber, tortoiseshell and jade at the far end of the room. While Liz and Sarah went with her to examine them, Lucinda was left alone with him beside the Hermes. To break the awkward silence between them he took down a small picture of Yorkshire moorland that hung above it and asked her if she thought Sarah would like it as a wedding present.

She hesitated. "So you think there will be a wedding?" she murmured.

"Of course. Don't you?"

"I do not know what to think." The dark eyes raised to his were suddenly troubled. "She is so much in love with him, but he is still at Eldon and he has not written to her once since he has been there. It does not look like devotion on his side, Edward."

"But I will not believe he will jilt her because she has lost her money."

"Do you not think so, when—" She broke off and went on in a calmer tone. "Gerald Dunfoyne says that Vincent is making bets with Rick Delamere that are beyond all reason."

"Is Dunfoyne there?"

"Yes. Frank had a letter from him this morning. Vincent told Gerald that he plans to win enough off Rick to pay his debts."

"He'll get in deeper if he doesn't look out. Fortune is seldom kind to the desperate."

"Now how can you know that?" Lucinda tried to laugh at him. "According to Frank, the only bets you ever make are on the rare occasions when he can persuade you to attend prize fights!"

"Frank does not know everything."

"And do you know more from the pages of your books?" She gave a small sigh. "I think you may be right all the same. Vincent may well come back poorer than when he went."

"I wonder that Dunfoyne is at Eldon. I should not have thought his pocket deep enough for the Eldon play."

"Oh, Gerald does not play with Rick and his friends. He has been invited solely to amuse the old gentleman with backgammon every night."

"You see a great deal of Mr. Dunfoyne?"

"He is a friend of Frank's." She met his coolness with lightness. "I wonder you do not know him better considering how well you knew his sister in Rome." And then as Maria joined them she continued, goading him unmercifully, "We are talking about the Dunfoynes— Edward admires Clara so much you know."

Edward disregarded her teasing and asked his sister's

opinion of the Yorkshire moors for Sarah's wedding present. She allowed that it was pretty, but the cameos were better. So Sarah selected a small, beautifully carved Persephone on tortoiseshell, and then Edward conducted them to the dining parlor, where wine and cake was provided for their refreshment. The wine was excellent but the cake was deplorable, and the girls abused it laughingly, saying it was small wonder that he was so thin.

Before they left he showed them the rest of his small domain, and they admired the main staircase with its walls decorated with painted wreaths of flowers—a souvenir of the French emigrés. They admired too the paneled parlor on the ground floor that he had turned into a small library, and the garden with its yew hedges, and the greenhouse where he hoped to grow pines, and the stables where there was room for six horses, his own gig and a traveling coach, if that was necessary.

"And what would be the use of a traveling coach to you?" asked Maria. "I must tell you, Lucinda, that my brother Edward usually travels by mail."

"He travels that way for speed!" Liz defended him stoutly. "He has told me all about it. If you are in a private carriage and find yourself behind an old gentleman who wishes to spare his horses, you may have to go at a snail's pace for some miles before you can overtake him, may not you, Edward? Whereas nothing stops the mails; they pay no tolls and the toll-keepers come running to open the gates directly they catch the first sound of the horn."

"Liz makes it sound like an adventure!" said Lucinda, laughing.

"Edward will never travel like a gentleman," said Maria.

"He is like nobody else in the world," said little Liz, clasping her arms about him.

"I daresay Vincent and I will often travel by stage-coach or mail in the future," said Sarah cheerfully. "Because I am sure we shall not have the means to do otherwise."

Lucinda said she thought it was time they set off for Richmond.

Rick Delamere had no hesitation in telling Vincent that he was a fool to continue with his engagement.

"A plain wife," he said one night in his friend's room, after a session at cards during which Mr. Chevening's debts had risen alarmingly, "is only possible if there is a fortune attached to her, and in your case, with the fortune gone, surely you cannot face the prospect of sitting opposite Miss Wakefield at breakfast for the rest of your life? You cannot admire her, my dear fellow. She has the face of a Yorkshire sheep."

"I have never admired her." Vincent's words were slightly blurred because he had drunk deep of old Mr. Delamere's claret. "But I admired her money."

"All the same, if you wish to rid yourself of the young lady you will have to act quickly. The wedding is scarcely a week away. If I were you I'd sit down and write her a letter at once, breaking the whole thing off."

"Break the whole thing off," repeated Vincent solemnly, nodding. He sat down at the writing table in the room and took a sheet of paper out of the drawer. "But what shall I say?" he asked stupidly.

"Let me mend one of those pens for you and I will tell you." Rick took a pen from the pen-holder, mended it quickly and dipped it in the inkwell. He held it out to his friend, who took it passively and sat waiting for him to proceed.

"Dear Miss Wakefield," dictated Rick.

"But I call her Sarah—or Sal. Always have done." Vincent looked at him owlishly.

"Do you wish to end the engagement or do you not?" asked Rick impatiently. "If you are not formal in the way you address her she will think that you do not mean what you say. Write as I tell you."

"Dear Miss Wakefield," Vincent wrote obediently, and the letter that followed was so short that it did not strain his powers of concentration overmuch. *"I do not see any possibility for me to continue in my engagement to marry you, and must end it without any further delay. A plain woman with money is acceptable, but without it she is intolerable. Yours sincerely, V. Chevening"*

"There," said Mr. Delamere when he had done. "That is finished. You are free now to find another heiress and there are plenty of pretty ones about." He took the letter, folded it, and after it was addressed, sealed it with Vincent's seal. "We will not trust it to a servant, but you can post it yourself in Eldon tomorrow. In fact I will race you across the Common to celebrate your freedom."

"Done," said Vincent.

The next morning he woke with a rather guilty sense of having done something of which his conscience vaguely did not approve, but it was easily appeased when he considered that it had only been Sarah's money that had attracted him to her, and therefore she could not blame him for breaking off their engagement.

His head was aching fiercely from the effects of the night's drinking. Few of the other guests were visible in the breakfast room, but Rick was there and full of the race before them.

"You will take your bays," he said, "and I will take my blacks. My curricle is heavier than yours so you will have to give me five minutes' start."

Vincent viewed the chops his friend was eating with distaste and sliced himself some cold tongue. "How far do you propose we should go?" he asked. "Down the Portsmouth road?"

"Good God, no. It is as full of traffic as the Brighton run. We'll cut across the Common where there's a flat surface and a wide road. We'll start from the milestone this end and finish four miles away at that small wood beyond the bridge as you come up into Eldon village."

"I'm ready to bet a thousand," boasted Vincent, encouraged by a stiff brandy and water that had accompanied the cold tongue, "that my bays will beat your blacks, and with a five-minutes' start."

"A thousand!" Rick laughed. "Make it twenty and I'm your man."

"Make it twenty then," said Vincent recklessly.

The curricles were brought round, and by the time a few of the stragglers from a party that had lasted well into the morning had gathered for breakfast, it was almost time to start. The bet was noted gravely by young Dunfoyne, who had not drunk as much as the others and was therefore well able to focus his attention on what was going forward, which he did with misgiving, knowing Delamere and suspecting trickery somewhere.

He rode with them to the first milestone on the Common, and when he gave the signal to start Delamere set off at speed. When, five minutes later, the lighter curricle started off he was almost out of sight, going a tremendous pace.

Vincent took his whip and lashed at the bays until they caught up with the blacks and passed them, although they had to mount the Common to do so, Delamere holding the center of the road and refusing to give way.

Vincent then took the crown of the road in his turn, but a few minutes later he heard the thunder of hoofs behind him and the whinnying of the blacks as Rick's vicious whip reached them. They passed him, mounting the Common as he had been forced to do. The two young men kept on across the Common in this way, passing and repassing and going hell for leather, often nearly over-turned by the uneven surface of the land. Hookey, Vincent's groom, hung on to his hat and to the side of the curricle, thinking every moment must be his last, but his protests were drowned in his master's shouts as he pursued the blacks and in Rick's answering jeers as he passed them again and again.

The miles sped away in this fashion until a belt of trees appeared beyond a bridge at the top of a rise. The bridge spanned a small stream, and it was only when he was too near to stop that Vincent saw that the approach to it nar-rowed, allowing only one vehicle to pass over at a time. He was slightly ahead, however, and he put on a spurt and laughed to think that the twenty thousand was as good as in his pocket. It did not occur to him that Rick would attempt to overtake him in such a narrow space until Hookey suddenly shouted to him to pull to the right.

"He's coming up be'ind us, sir, at the devil's own lick," he yelled. "And he's on the wrong side of the road."

"He cannot pass me on the bridge," Vincent shouted back. "And I'll be there before him."

The bridge, however, was humpbacked; the road rose steeply toward it and on either side the ground fell away to flat meadowland, where cattle were grazing peacefully beside a meandering stream. As Vincent drove the bays up the narrow rise to the bridge the blacks were suddenly beside him, and Rick Delamere pulled on the reins, drawing his horses sharply across his opponent's in a way contrary to all rules of the road.

Swearing at him, Vincent pulled over to the right, where the off-wheels of his curricle slipped and slid over the grass verge. Then the fancy carriage broke through the bars of the protecting fence and plunged down to the meadow thirty feet below.

Drawing up on the far side of the bridge with a shout of triumph Rick looked over his shoulder and saw the gap in the fence and the empty road. He threw the reins to his man and ran back, and the groom, having secured the blacks to a tree, went after him.

They arrived to see the curricle upside down, with one wheel off and the coachwork splintered. Hookey, who had managed to jump clear, was slashing at the harness, trying to free the bays.

Vincent was unable to help. He was lying beneath the shattered remains of his beautiful new curricle with a broken neck.

His heir's death was a blow from which Sir William did not recover easily, but on the question of where he was to be buried the baronet stood firm. Accompanied by Edward, he had the body removed to Chevening and buried in the family vault, and when Sophia protested he said that it was his eldest son's right to be there.

"He should be at Edgecombe," cried Sophia. "All the children were born there and it is our real home."

"We have taken him to Chevening, my love, where his family is." He urged her to leave London and go with the girls to Edgecombe. "There will be many things to arrange here and in Chevening, and Edward will assist me."

"I hope he will think less of his stupid collection now that he is your heir," Sophia said bitterly.

"Nobody could have been of greater help." It was Edward for whom his father had sent when the news of Vincent's death reached them, and he had come directly, bringing Tod with him and taking all that he could from Sir William's shoulders. Tod had not been without his uses either; while they were at Eldon he had visited the inn yard in the little market town to save the remains of the curricle from the bonfire. The bays had been sent to the knacker's yard on the day of the accident, and Hookey brought the silver-mounted whip and harness and the new reins to Tod, saying that he intended to give up private service. "I'd rather sit be'ind a team in a London wagon," he told him bitterly, "than see beautiful h'animals killed wantonly for the sake of young gentlemen's wagers."

Neither Sir William nor his wife held Rick Delamere responsible for the accident that had killed their son. "I've seldom seen a man more cut up than Delamere was," Sir William told Sophia. "He said that Vincent attempted to pass him on the bridge and although he did his best to check him he forced his way past, and in so doing went over the parapet. I am convinced it was not Rick's fault."

"No, it was not his fault." Sophia said that she knew from what Jasper let out that Vincent had a few debts.

"I daresay he thought this stupid wager would be a way of paying them off before his marriage."

The debts, Sir William thought grimly, could scarcely be a few if the wager he had made to clear them was twenty thousand pounds.

"You will feel better when you are at Edgecombe," he told her. "And Jasper's captain will grant him leave to go with you and the girls."

"I cannot take Sarah," she said. "Don't think me a heartless wretch, Will, dearest. Indeed I am not heartless where poor Sarah is concerned. I am sure it has been a terrible shock for her, but she is young and she will recover and marry someone else. In the meantime I must separate myself from her sad little face. I sometimes wish that we had never taken her into our home."

Her husband remembered how the same thought had come to him, but for a different reason, when Sarah had become engaged to Vincent, and he asked Sophia if she would like him to sound Lady Stroud over it. "She might care to take her back to Chevening with her when she goes," he said.

"Oh, if she would!" For the first time in days the warm look came back to her eyes. "Oh, Will, that would be a most excellent solution!"

That evening after dinner he took his sister aside and put the question to her. "The long and the short of it is this, Minnie. Sophia has got it into her head that she does not want Sarah at Edgecombe. A great piece of nonsense, of course, but one cannot expect her to be reasonable yet."

"It is the shock of Vincent's death," Lady Stroud assured him. "When she gets over it a little she will welcome her into your family circle as warmly as ever. Let me take Sarah back with me by all means, and while we are on the subject, Will dear, much as I love Chevening Place I would like to remove from it as soon as possible."

"You wish to leave Chevening?" He could not believe it.

"Not Chevening, dear, only the Place. Chevening Lodge in the village would suit me admirably. It is quite sufficient for my needs, and it has a nice garden. A couple of gardeners would be all I should require. I feel that it is time for you to take possession of the Place and to manage the estate as your father did before you, with your excellent agent, Mr. Belton, to help you."

Although unwilling to press her brother at such a time, she reminded him that when her husband was alive he had been pleased to undertake Sir William's duties for him with Mr. Belton, but such duties were beyond her own powers. "You and Sophia have had many happy years in your charming little manor house, Will, and I feel you should move to Chevening now and make it your home."

There was sense in what she said, and as he remained silent she continued: "Dearest Sophia will be depressed for some years to come, but it is better for her to leave a house where every corner must remind her of Vincent and start afresh at Chevening."

In the meantime she agreed to set out for Kent with Sarah on the day that Sophia, with her daughters and Jasper, took the Bath road to Edgecombe.

Seven

After they were all gone the great London mansion seemed empty and desolate. The servants moved about quietly with grave faces, and the baronet's rooms were the only ones in use. The glittering chandeliers were enclosed in holland covers, more covers hid the furniture, druggets were laid over Aubusson carpets, and brocade curtains were taken down and stored in chests with Chevening lavender.

Sir William was glad to have Edward continually with him, occupied as they both were with Vincent's affairs. The baronet had guessed his eldest son's debts to be large, but he had not dreamed what the final account would be. Not only were there twenty thousand pounds to be paid to Rick Delamere, and another thirty thousand in other debts of honor, but by the time Brayford had all the tradesmens' bills in Vincent's father found himself liable for another hundred thousand pounds.

"One hundred and fifty thousand pounds—one third of the value of the Chevening estates!" In his grief and anger he asked accusingly if Edward had known what had been going on.

Edward said that Vincent had not confided in him, but that he and Jasper had been concerned about him, thinking that he might be plunging too deeply. Sir William then apologized for his outburst. He found his second son more of a help in those dark days than he would ever have thought possible, he had in fact a fine intelligence and a quick grasp of practical matters that his father found invaluable. He agreed with him now that although some of the estate must go, there was timber at Chevening that would fetch a good price in the nation's shipyards.

Edward went down to Chevening Place, and with Mr. Bolton he pored over maps and went through the accounts and the income that the tenants brought into the estate office. They conducted their discussions in the small library after dinner rather than in the office during the day, where the agent had a succession of visitors in tenant farmers, head carpenters, stone masons, builders, herdsmen, thatchers, water bailiffs and game-keepers, and many others employed in keeping cottages neat and watertight, farm-houses in trim, fences mended and land drained, and in preserving game in the coverts and fish in the rivers.

The home farm, too, took up a certain amount of time. Sir William owned some prize cattle that he did not wish to part with, and at the end of several weeks of discussion Edward was able to return to London to tell his father with encouraging cheerfulness that although the Chevening estate must shrink, it would still remain comparatively large and profitable if certain entrenchments could be made in the family's expenditure. He thought Lady Stroud's suggestion that they should move to Chevening excellent and advised the letting of Edgecombe.

"Your mother would never consent to that." But Sir William agreed that the house in St. James's Square should be sold and a smaller one purchased or rented instead. He said he would go to Edgecombe the following week to talk it over with Edward's mother, while his son returned to Chevening to decide with Mr. Belton on the sale of the timber and land that must go.

Compared with Edgecombe, Chevening Place was immense. The old house had been pulled down by Sir William's grandfather in the middle of the previous century, and a large Palladian mansion had taken its place.

The two lodges at the main entrance were joined by a large central arch, and through the gates beneath it could be seen the road, leading between the oaks until it left them, sweeping round past the stable block to the house itself.

The entrance to the house was in the North front, a portico with a triangular pediment and wide steps of Portland stone leading to the entrance to the main block, two wings built of the same stone spreading out on either side to form a house that might have been taken from an Italian landscape rather than the more homely one of England. And yet so fine were its proportions that it did not look out of place in the English hills. On the South side Italian gardens had been planned in terraces, stepping down to the park fence with the lake in the valley beyond. That the water of the lake was often a steely blue under grey skies and the cattle and sheep that grazed there very English cattle and sheep, fitted into an outstandingly English landscape.

Great rooms led from the large, marble-floored hall one into another: private sitting rooms into dressing rooms, state bedrooms and libraries into dining rooms, the green drawing room into the rose drawing room; and, finally, there was the immense picture gallery, seventy-five feet long.

From the gallery walls the faces of past Chevenings looked down on their successor as Edward stood there looking up at them: some austere, some slightly disapproving, some frankly arrogant, and one very dashing cavalier who had fallen fighting for his king at Marston Moor. A Royalist lot, these Chevenings.

So thought Edward, wondering how his mother and the girls and Sarah would settle into this large, cold house after the cozy warmth of Edgecombe. When all was done he joined his father at Edgecombe Manor to obtain his consent to his and Belton's conclusions, but he did not stay longer than was necessary to complete the business. On the morning that he left, Liz came down to make his breakfast for him.

"Edward," she said hesitantly as she poured out his coffee, "may I speak to you rather seriously about something?"

"Of course, Liz. What is the matter?"

"I don't quite know how to say it . . . have I made your coffee as you like it?"

"It is delicious, thank you, my dear." He waited and after a moment she burst out: "Is it true that Vincent's debts have ruined Papa? That he is having to sell Chevening and the London house and—everything— and that there will only be Edgecombe left?"

"No, of course it is not true. Who put such an idea into your head?"

"Mary Fouldes."

"Mary Fouldes?" He frowned, trying to remember her; there were so many in the Fouldes family that he never could remember all their names.

"You must remember Mary. She is my dearest friend."

"Oh, I see." There was nothing like a dearest friend, he thought, for enjoying the misfortunes of her neighbors. "And what did Miss Fouldes have to say?"

"She had it from her papa, who had it from the rector, who had it from a gentleman in Bath—"

"That your papa was ruined?"

"Why yes." Liz looked at him hopefully.

"Then the next time you meet Miss Fouldes," he said, smiling, "you may tell her that her papa, and the rector and the gentleman in Bath are all equally mistaken. There is still to be a house in London for the family, my love, if a slightly smaller one, and Chevening is far from being sold, and your papa is a long way from ruin."

Liz drew a long sigh of relief. "I told Mary that I was sure she was wrong," she said. "But she was so positive, you know."

Edward knew only too well. It was a wet morning, and he glanced out the window at the dripping trees and the faded autumn colors and thought of his sisters cooped up there with their mother's grief. He was angry with Jasper for having stayed only a few weeks before going off to Melton Mowbray for the start of the fox-hunting season.

"It is now the beginning of November," he said. "If the family moves to Chevening Place before Christmas you will be near to London and you and Maria shall come on a visit to me in the spring." He knew that his mother would not consider a London Season for Liz and he was determined that she should have some enjoyment in her seventeenth year. "We will go to theaters," he went on, seeing the light in her eyes, "and I will arrange to give parties for you and invite some of my friends to meet you. We will go to concerts, and I will hire a little carriage to take you about in, and if Maria prefers to go shopping you shall come by yourself."

"Oh, Edward!" She hugged him, nearly spilling his coffee. "But Maria will come—I know she will—and not only for the shopping, though she will adore that. Oh, my dearest Edward, we will look forward to it so much and it will cheer us through the months ahead. Please take us to that nice house of yours as soon as you can."

She saw him go with much more cheerfulness, and after the carriage had taken him off to catch the nine o'clock coach from Bath she ran upstairs to tell Maria what was in store for them.

The move from Edgecombe to Chevening was finally decided when Sophia told her husband that she had asked the rector of Edgecombe to dinner one evening to discuss where the memorial tablet was to be placed in the church.

"The memorial tablet, my dear? What memorial tablet?" asked Sir William mildly.

"Why, in memory of Vincent. I have decided that it shall be made of Bath stone—very simply worded, just stating that he was the eldest son of Sir William Chevening of Edgecombe Manor, and his age when he died." She glanced uneasily at him. "But you must see to the wording of it yourself, of course, and discuss it with the rector tonight."

"I shall be pleased to see the rector," he said quietly, "but not to discuss memorial tablets with him. I have already arranged to have a memorial made at Chevening. Edward has recommended an excellent sculptor who will carve a profile from the miniature Vincent had done for Sarah. It is in Edward's possession now. Chevening is our home, my dear, not Edgecombe, which only came to me through my mother's uncle. It has nothing to do with the Chevenings. Chevening Place has been in the family for centuries, long before my grandfather pulled down the old house. Minnie was right, it is time we made our home there again, and I shall write to her tonight and tell her to put her own move to Chevening Lodge in hand as soon as possible."

He saw the protest in his wife's face, and he told himself that Vincent's death must not separate them. He came to her and put his arm round her. "I know you have never liked Chevening, but it is the right thing to do, my love, and in your heart you know it as well as I do."

"It is Edward who has put this into your mind," she said resentfully.

"No, you shall not blame Edward for this. It is entirely between you and me—and Minnie."

The sales of the property and timber at Chevening were only the beginning of the economies that were necessary before Sir William felt he could hold up his head and look the world in the face.

The large mansion in St. James's Square was exchanged for a pleasant house in Dover Street, selected by Edward as being suitable in size and in its appurtenances. The number of rooms was sufficient for the family and for the entertainment of friends, if not on the lavish scale of St. James's. Every room was wainscoted and even the windows of the servants' garrets were glazed with Crown glass. The octagonal skylight had eight Ionic columns, carved capitals and balusters, and a flower in plaster at the top of the skylight. It is true that the festoons of fruit and flowers over the doors of the rooms and on the staircase walls might be of plaster instead of carved wood, and it was equally true that the treads of the staircase, though wide and shallow, were of oak instead of marble, but the porter's hall was floored with Portland stone, as were the steward's room, a lodging for servants, wine vaults, a servants' hall, a laundry and a butler's pantry, and at the end of the garden sufficient stabling and coach houses for the family's needs.

Sir William had never had to consider money before, but he was beginning to realize that had Vincent lived, in a very short while there would have been nothing left. He dispatched the carriages and horses that could not be accommodated in Dover Street to Chevening, sending one closed carriage to Sloane Street for Edward's use.

"It will save you from getting wet on winter nights," he told his son, and with the thought of his sisters' visit in the spring Edward accepted it in the spirit in which it was given, and had it stored next to his gig.

The move was completed before Christmas, Edgecombe being left in the hands of a steward and a housekeeper. Since it was to be a strange Christmas for them all in the unaccustomed surroundings of the Place, which until then had been visited by Lady Chevening and her family only during the summer months, Frank Crayne and his sister were invited to join them there.

The girls were fond of Lucinda, and her gaiety and spirits brought life into the great, unfamiliar house. Frank too brought a brighter air with him, and they were glad of his company.

Clara Dunfoyne was home from Rome. That autumn she had become engaged to the Honorable John Moresby, the heir to Lord Moresby, whose estates adjoined those of Chevening. It was not long, therefore, before the numbers at Chevening were increased nearly every day by Gerald and Clara and John Moresby, usually bringing several young Moresbys with them.

Gerald Dunfoyne took up again his allegiance to Lucinda, and she encouraged him in a lighthearted way that Edward found irritating. The cool manner with which he treated her when they met Lucinda construed as indifference. She began to think that with the exception of Liz, the Chevenings had no hearts, and this was confirmed when she teased Clara one day about Edward's devotion to her in Rome.

"Edward!" Clara opened her blue eyes wide and laughed. "Edward never looked at a woman in his life. When he could be persuaded to remove himself from an art gallery it was to pursue Vincent to see that he was not at the card tables again. Poor Edward had a hard time of it, I fear."

"But Vincent said—" Lucinda broke off as Clara smiled.

"Surely you never believed anything he said?" she said, dropping her voice. "My dear Lucinda, he was the biggest liar in Rome. He made love to me outrageously, knowing all the time that he was going to engage himself to Miss Wakefield when he arrived home, but I can promise you I was never taken in by him for a moment.

He was shallow, vain and selfish, and where his heart should have been there was a stone."

The winter was a hard one, and the New Year came in with bitter weather and roads frozen so that even the walk to Chevening village a mile away was often impossible.

The Dunfoynes made nothing of it, however, and the Moresby carriages brought them time and again to indulge in noisy games of commerce or loo or lottery, or else they would gather round the pianoforte in the music room, where Lucinda played and sang ballads. When snow threatened to cut them off, the young men of the party had the sleighs out and the horses shod in felt to take them through the snowy roads in the moonlight to dances and dinners, the girls muffled in fur mantles and declaring themselves to be as frozen as the streams in the meadows.

In all these festivities, however, one thing struck Lucinda as odd: Sarah Wakefield was not included in their parties, and when Lady Stroud visited the Place she did not accompany her.

One fine frosty morning, Frank and Jasper having gone duck shooting with John Moresby and Gerald Dunfoyne, Clara being confined to Moresby with a cold, and Maria and Liz having no desire to venture out, Lucinda announced her intention of walking down to Chevening Lodge to see Sarah. Edward, finding himself free from estate business for once, offered to accompany her. As they started out she asked him why Sarah never came to the Place.

"Perhaps she thinks it would bring back memories," he said, never having really considered it before.

"I do not believe it," said Lucinda stoutly. "What, a sensible little creature like Sarah wearing the willow for the rest of her life! She is only eighteen."

"She was very much in love with my brother," he reminded her.

"I daresay she was, poor child, but from something Liz said yesterday I had the impression that she was no longer welcome at Chevening Place. Is that the reason why she avoids you all? Lady Stroud is a dear, good woman but surely younger company would be better for Sarah sometimes?"

Edward said he thought they must leave that to Sarah to decide. "As for her not being welcome in the family," he added, "if Liz gave you that impression it was totally wrong."

"Yet when it was suggested that your aunt should dine with us last Sunday your mother said that she did not suppose Sarah would come. Is it not time that somebody made an effort to bring her back into the family, Edward?"

He had to admit that he had not thought of Sarah as often as he should. On the occasions when he had visited the lodge she had been out walking, or occupied in another room.

"Well, I have something in my muff that should comfort her a little," Lucinda said, smiling. "Though it may cause an added sadness as well." She told him that Mr. Delamere's man had found a letter addressed to Sarah in Vincent's coat pocket after the accident and had asked Gerald Dunfoyne to give it to her. "As Gerald does not know her very well I have been employed as his postboy this morning."

"Mr. Dunfoyne does not hesitate to employ his friends in delicate matters," said Edward.

"Oh, but I have known Gerald for a long time," protested Lucinda warmly. "He is a charming young man and I am very fond of him."

Edward remarked that it had not escaped his notice. "Do you plan to marry him?" he asked in a voice so unconcerned that she felt she hated him.

"It is difficult to make up my mind," she said with the affectation that he detested. "On the one hand, he has the future title that my uncle wishes for me, but the fortune is lacking. The Dunfoynes are so poor."

"It does not appear to have influenced Moresby," he said.

"Ah, but then Clara is so enchanting, is she not?"

His answer was not one to please her. "Her simplicity is certainly engaging in these days of insincerity."

Her flippancy was silenced for a moment, and he asked her if she knew what was in the letter.

"Why no, but I would hazard that it is a love letter, would not you?"

"A love letter? From Vincent?" Edward did not believe it. "I think you would be wiser to burn it unread."

"What do you mean?" She was uneasily reminded of Clara's warning. "Do you imagine, just because you are so cold, that Vincent was incapable of writing love letters?"

"My feelings have nothing to do with it," he replied. "But I have come to know my brother's character better since he died than I did in his lifetime. That letter may stir up more than you imagine, Lucinda, and I sincerely advise you not to give it to Sarah."

"And I think you must allow me, as a woman, to judge for myself over that," retorted Lucinda, putting her head in the air.

"Certainly." He said no more until they reached Chevening Lodge, and when she asked if he were coming in with her he replied that his aunt would not forgive him if he did not.

Lady Stroud welcomed them kindly, and told them that Sarah had awakened with a bad headache and had been persuaded to stay in bed. Lucinda said she would go up and see her and left Edward with his aunt. She found Sarah dressed and sitting in a chair by the window, watching a country wagon making slow progress along the frosty road. As Lucinda entered she turned languidly to greet her, and gave her a hand that trembled and was burning hot.

"Sarah," Lucinda said with concern, her affectation dropping from her like a cloak, "you are not well!"

"I am quite well, thank you," said Sarah quietly. "Purchase has helped me to dress and I am better now. I shall soon feel able to go downstairs."

"Sarah, what is the matter?" Lucinda's dark eyes dwelt on her with compassion. "Is it Vincent's death—or is there something else troubling you? If there is, won't you tell me what?"

Sarah thought for a long moment and then said with a sigh, "As you are not one of the Chevenings there can be no harm in confiding in you. Lucinda, I think Vincent's mother hates me. I believe she holds me responsible for his death."

"But that is noneense!" Lucinda's voice did not carry complete conviction, however. "What make you think such a thing? Surely Lady Chevening must be fonder of you than ever, knowing what you meant to Vincent."

"That might be a stranger's notion of her," said Sarah with a wan little smile. "But it would not be the truth."

"This at least should comfort you," said Lucinda. She took the letter from her muff, explaining where it had been found and that Gerald Dunfoyne had asked her to give it to Sarah. "Vincent's last love letter, my dearest."

"A love letter? From Vincent?" Tears started to Sarah's eyes, and she opened it eagerly. Then, as she read the few words in it she gave a gasp, a muffled cry, and slipped to the floor in a dead faint.

Lucinda ran for help, and Purchase and the house-keeper between them got her back to bed and restored her with burnt feathers and vinegar. When she opened her eyes it was to see Lucinda bending over her, her face full of concern.

"I should never have given you that letter," she said, full of self-reproach. "I should have kept it until you were strong enough to bear it."

"No. You did quite right. Give it to me, please." Sarah slipped the letter under her pillow, and as there was no more she could do Lucinda left her to the ministrations of Purchase and the housekeeper.

"It is my belief, miss," said the latter in a whisper as she saw her to the head of the stairs, "that poor young lady is in a decline. She eats no more than would feed a sparrow and she used to eat hearty, like the rest of the young ladies when they were here."

As she walked back with Edward, now equally concerned for Sarah, she admitted that she had been in the wrong. "You were right, Edward," she said, putting her hand apologetically on his sleeve. "I should have burnt the wretched letter rather than give it to her."

He took her hand and tucked it into his arm. "You did what you thought was right." He smiled down at her in the old warm way. "It may do her more good than we imagine."

In spite of the cold wind a few primroses had started to push up their leaves in the banks of the lane to Chevening Place and it would not be long before the catkins would show on the willows that overhung the streams. She was suddenly very glad that Gerald Dunfoyne had gone duck shooting that morning and that his sister Clara had stayed at home with a cold.

As for Edward, even the long shadow of Vincent for once lost its power to spoil the brightness of the morning.

Eight

The following morning, Edward and Jasper left for London. Frank and Lucinda were to leave for Crayne two days later. On the day before their departure, Lucinda walked down to the lodge to inquire after Sarah and found the invalid sitting up in bed feeling very much better.

"I hoped you would come," she said in her old energetic way. "I want you to read this—Vincent's love letter to his future wife!" She watched while Lucinda read it and noticed that she had to read it twice before she was able to assimilate its contents.

"But this is abominable!" she exclaimed. "It cannot have been from Vincent!"

"Oh yes," said Sarah calmly. "It is certainly from Vincent, and it has only confirmed what has been in my mind since I was banished from the family after his death. Sir William and Lady Chevening adopted me,

Lucinda, because of the fortune they hoped would pass from me to one of their sons. Vincent was the obvious choice and I was encouraged to admire him and to think myself in love with him—indeed I *was* in love with him. But once my fortune was gone I was no longer wanted, and this letter of Vincent's, cruel as it is, only echoes what was in his parents' minds. I was in fact a bad bargain, where in the past I had been a good one." She clenched her fist and beat it fiercely on her bed. "Lucinda, I mean to leave Chevening and sever all ties with the family. I mean to put such a distance between us that I need never hear their names or see their faces again."

"What are you going to do?"

"I think there may be some of my mother's relatives still living in or near Corrieford. I am not entirely penniless: Wakefield House can be sold, and the money properly invested should give me a small competence of my own." The shrewd business sense of her Yorkshire father here showed itself. "I have written to Mr. Adams and I have told him what I have told you—that now I have no fortune I am no longer welcome in Vincent's family, that I am unhappy here and wish to make my home with some relative in Yorkshire, if there are any who would give me shelter. I have asked him to send a reply to be called for at the Chevening post office, and I want you to take my letter there and send it off on your way home, Lucinda."

"But of course I will." Lucinda took it from her gladly.

"Now that I have a hope of leaving Chevening," Sarah said cheerfully, "I shall grow strong again, and I shall not forget you, Lucinda. You have been my only real friend."

Lucinda tried to remind her that Liz and Edward had

always been attached to her, but she would have none of it. "No Chevening is a friend of mine," she said.

As she started out on her journey to Crayne with her brother, Lucinda wondered if she were not right. After the cruelty of Vincent's letter she found herself wishing to get away from Chevening herself. Into the family's expressions of regret at their departure she thought she had read relief that they were going, and when Lady Chevening said she hoped they would soon see them again she wondered if the opposite was not the case. Clara Dunfoyne had put a doubt into her mind and Sarah's outburst had strengthened it. She could no longer believe in their sincerity, and she was thankful to be on her way to the cold discomfort of Crayne.

On hearing of Sarah's fainting fit, Sophia Chevening had been conscience-stricken, and she was careful to include Sarah by name in her next invitation to dinner at the Place. Sarah came and was very composed and formal: "Aunt Sophia" had now become "Lady Connington," and "Uncle Will" was "Sir William." She took their inquires after her health with tranquility: she was quite well again now, she thought that perhaps the cold weather had affected her, and she was sorry she had not felt well enough to visit them at Christmas. She might have been an acquaintance who had never been on close terms with any of them.

After she had gone Sophia complained that her manner had bordered on the impertinent. "I hope she does not intend to forget all you have done for her," she told her husband indignantly. "It would be abominably ungrateful in her if she did."

"I do not think Sarah is ungrateful," said Sir William

thoughtfully. He too had been puzzled by the girl's manner. "A great deal of it may stem from uncertainty; she may be trying to discover where she now stands in our family."

As the days went by Sarah no longer avoided the Chevening girls when they called at the lodge but, although pleasant and well-mannered, she held them, too, at arms' length.

And then one day Lucinda received a letter from her to say that Mr. Adams had replied to her inquiries. He told her that Sarah had a grandfather living, a farmer by the name of Hargreaves, and that he had sent one of his clerks out to Thistlethwaite Farm to see the old gentleman and to show him her letter. Mr. Hargreaves had been delighted to have news of his granddaughter and promised to write to her himself directly the lambing was over.

"I do hope he will write soon and offer me a home with him at Thistlethwaite," Sarah wrote. *"Isn't it a lovely name?"*

The letter was so happy that Lucinda's heart misgave her. There had been no mention of the old gentleman giving Sarah a home. Supposing he was merely putting her off with his talk of lambing and had no intention of doing anything for her? Supposing in fact that he did not keep his promise to write?

With the problems this presented she found her distrust of the Chevenings growing. If any of them possessed a heart under their charming manners, she argued, Sarah would still be regarded as a daughter at Chevening Place. She determined to think of them no more.

They were now in the middle of February, and Edward returned to Kent before the end of the month to make arrangements for his sisters to visit him at the beginning of April. The girls were delighted but their mother raised an objection that fortunately was soon to be overcome.

"You have no lady in your house, Edward. I do not think your sisters should stay there with you alone."

"I do not see why they should not. I am their brother and I assure you I shall devote my entire time to their entertainment during their stay." He hesitated. "Will you not come with them, Mamma?"

"No, I could not enjoy theaters and evening parties yet." Vincent's shadow was there again between them, reminding her of how much he had enjoyed theaters.

"I beg your pardon, ma'am. I was thinking of my sisters."

"I know you were. You are a kindhearted fellow, Edward, if thoughtless at times. And I would like the poor girls to have their visit to you. I wonder if your Aunt Stroud would not go in my place. Walk down there this morning, my dear, and ask her."

He took his sisters with him to make their request to his aunt, and she did not hesitate for a moment. She would be charmed to accompany the girls, she told them; they had had little gaiety since Christmas and she would bring Sarah. It would be quite like old times.

He said he would be delighted to welcome Sarah in his house, and without giving him time to continue, Lady Stroud went on, "I can see a certain amount of conjecture in your face, Edward. You are wondering how you will cram us all into your small house, because of course there will be Purchase, and the girls' maid Tully, and as I shall travel in my own comfortable carriage there will be my men-servants and my horses to be accommodated."

He assured her that they would manage perfectly. "We

thought it all out as we walked down here from the Place. You, my dear aunt, will have my room, with Purchase in the dressing room next door. I will have a tent-bed on the floor above, and the three girls will share a room that was once a young ladies' dormitory in the days when the house was a school."

"And the servants?"

"My cook and housemaids sleep in the garret and the girls' maid can join them there. The men-servants can have the lodging room next to Tod's in the kitchen area under the house. So you see there will be no difficulty at all."

"I trust your cook has improved since the last time I dined with you?" Only once had Lady Stroud dined with her nephew, and the boiled fowl that had been served on that occasion had been almost worse than the onion sauce with which it had been smothered.

"As my digestion does not suffer as much as it did I conclude that she has improved." He added as a recommendation that she pickled cucumbers very well.

"I will risk it, then," said her ladyship, as his sisters laughed. "You may tell your mother, Maria, that I shall call on her tomorrow morning to discuss your visit and that I intend to bring you all to London in the first week in April. My carriage is quite large enough to hold us, as long as Purchase and Tully travel outside, and if Purchase does not enjoy it I daresay Tully will, my footman being young, unmarried and good-looking."

Edward thought that in such a situation it was an excellent thing that Tully should be lodged in the garret and the footman in the kitchen quarters. He thanked her for her help and walked back with his sisters, delighted now that their visit was assured.

"I am glad," said Lady Stroud after the young people had gone, "that Lady Chevening confides in Edward more than she did."

"Did she never confide in him before then, ma'am?"

"Not very often, I am afraid. Vincent was her favorite."

"But that was scarcely Edward's fault, was it?" suggested Sarah, busy with a feather with which she was decorating one of her ladyship's hats.

"Many of us, my dear, have to suffer from what has not been our fault," said her companion, and began to talk about the hat in Sarah's hands. "It was the one that I wore for the Coronation," she told her. "Turbans were very popular that year." Her thoughts went back to the fat new king in his heavy robes driving to the color and pageantry of the Abbey, and the cheering crowds in the streets, the day only marred by the thought of the Queen, beating on the Abbey doors that were closed against her, paying for her sins and follies as her husband paid for his in the knowledge of her humiliation. "It is a terrible thing for a man when he is brought up in an atmosphere of dislike. Our present king was so hated by his parents that some think that is why he behaved as he did to his wife."

Sarah appeared to have no interest in His Majesty or in his consort, and Lady Stroud's thoughts went back to Sophia and her second son. From the time he was a child Edward had been old Lady Chevening's favorite, and she knew that Sophia had secretly resented it. She had never been fond of her husband's mother, and this lack of affection had been reciprocated. Although both ladies had treated each other with civility and respect they had been grateful for the miles that separated Chevening from Edgecombe.

But it was of no use to think about the past; the present was here and the future just around the corner. Lady Stroud asked what dresses her young companion planned to take to London.

"Those I wore at last year's balls, ma'am." Sarah showed no great interest in the subject.

"You will not allow me to give you some new ones?"

"By no means. The gowns I have are good enough for any occasion."

Minnie said no more. When she paid her morning call at the Place on the following day, however, she found there was something more important on Sophia's mind than her daughters' London visit. She said that she had received a letter that morning from her cousin, Henrietta St. Clair. "You remember her, I am sure, Minnie. Dearest Vincent visited her in France at the start of his tour with Edward."

"Oh yes. I do not think I have ever met her, but she lives in Paris, does she not?"

"Yes. Her husband will never leave his old château near Lyons, and dearest Vincent told me it was the ugliest as well as the most uncomfortable building he had ever visited. Henrietta has written to say that she had only just heard about the accident and to condole with us all for our tragic loss, which is kind of her because she is a very distant cousin of mine and I never knew a great deal about the family. It appears, however, that her daughter Ann-Marie is to marry a man from the new aristocracy in France, and Henrietta is coming to England in May to arrange for her dowry. I daresay her family have property that may be disposed of, but she does not mention that. She says that a friend has loaned her a house in Brighton for the summer, and she would be delighted if our two girls would join her there. Ann-Marie will be in Lyons with her father, but she thinks a change of air and scene might be good for Maria and Liz. I must say I think it extremely civil of her to write so kindly."

Lady Stroud agreed. "And you will let them go?" she asked.

"I have not quite made up my mind: the sea air would be beneficial, and although I do not care for the social life of Brighton, His Majesty is not likely to be there."

"His Majesty cares nothing for young girls, in any case," said Lady Stroud, smiling. "And I do not think he will spare a glance for Mme. St. Clair either as long as Lady Conyngham is there to keep him in good humor." Then as her sister-in-law still looked uncertain, she asked if there was any other reason why the girls should not go. Lady Chevening confessed that there was.

"Lady Harriet Delamere has a house in Brighton," she said, "and in the old days I believe she was a close friend of Henrietta's. Rick Delamere often visits his mother there."

"Mr. Delamere?" Lady Stroud frowned.

"I know what you are thinking, Minnie," said her sister-in-law. "And although I believe he had a bad influence over poor Vincent, the wager that led to the accident was only the stupid one that young men of our class make every day of their lives. Rick was not to know how important it was to Vincent that he should win it. But that is another matter. Last summer in London Rick paid a great deal of attention to Maria, and the foolish girl declared herself to be desperately in love with him."

"Has she seen him since?"

"Only when he has called here, which he has done once or twice on his way to Brighton."

If Lady Stroud thought Kent to be rather out of the way for Brighton, she did not say so. "Mr. Delamere has the reputation of being unprincipled and profligate," she said. "But I do not suppose the attentions he paid to Maria were more than he would have paid to any other pretty girl who happened to be a titled man's daughter. I am sorry Maria thought herself to be in love with him. Was she serious?"

"I hope not, but when I begged her to moderate her manners toward him she said he had an interesting pallor!"

"A pallor no doubt caused by his excesses," said Lady Stroud. "So many young men these days appear to emulate Lord Byron that one can only hope they are not as bad as they make themselves out to be."

"Byron." Sophia drew down her mouth. "Edward has a great admiration for his poetry."

"There is a melancholy in *Childe Harold* that might suit his mood. I wonder that Edward is not more popular with young ladies if an interesting pallor is what they admire."

"He has always been pale." Sophia dismissed her second son impatiently. She walked to the windows of her sitting room and looked out at the terraced gardens and stone fountains that stepped down to the park and the great lake in the valley below, her thoughts on the family who had lived there down the centuries. During the months since Vincent's death she had begun to appreciate the importance of the great house and to realize also its importance to her husband. To Sir William, the house as well as the estate was a sacred charge to be handed on intact to his heir—that heir now being the bookish Edward instead of her darling Vincent.

She turned from the prospect outside with a sigh. "There is one comfort to be found in the girls' visit to Edward. Cramped and uncomfortable as you will undoubtedly be, Mr. Delamere is not likely to visit Sloane Street."

"I promise you I will be a dragon, guarding the door against him," said Minnie, laughing. "Unless he is a friend of Edward's too?"

"Edward does not like him and Liz detests him, but I fear that Maria may be even more attracted to him than she was last summer. Neither Will nor I would welcome him as a son-in-law." She changed the subject abruptly. "Is Sarah going with you?"

Lady Stroud said that she was, but as things turned out she was mistaken, because a week later Miss Wakefield had a visitor with other plans for her.

Nine

Lady Stroud had just finished breakfast that morning, and she and her young companion were sitting in the morning room at the lodge wondering if it would be fine enough to take the carriage into Tunbridge Wells to see her ladyship's milliner, when a footman came to tell them that a gentleman was there to speak with Miss Wakefield.

"A gentleman to see you, child? Who can it be at this hour of the morning?" Without giving Sarah time to reply Lady Stroud supplied the answer herself. "It will be somebody from Mr. Brayford about a new tenant for your house. You may see him in the drawing room, my dear, while I speak to Mrs. Flitton."

The housekeeper was sent for to the morning room and the visitor was shown into the drawing room, where Sarah joined him a few seconds later. He was a large gentleman dressed in country-made clothes of good broadcloth, and he wore a beaver hat beneath which his whiskered face looked as red as if he had only that moment come off the Yorkshire moors. Directly she saw him she knew who he was.

"I am Miss Wakefield," she said, her heart beating fast. "Are you—can you be—"

"Your grandfather? Aye, if you be Sarah Wakefield, I am that." His great hands took her gently by the shoulders and held her at arms' length. "By gum, you're a bonny lass," he said. "Like your mother was at your age." He enfolded her in a bearlike hug, kissed her, and then with his arm round her waist he took her to a settee and sat down with her there comfortably.

"So Lady Stroud has been kind enough to give my granddaughter a home," he said. "I am very grateful to her for that, but I have come to take you home with me, my lass, if thou'rt willing to come and leave all this finery behind." He studied her with affectionate concern. "I'm a farmer and the life in my house is a busy one, not for fine ladies. But my daughter—that's your mother's sister Ruth, that keeps house for me—gave me a message that she would welcome you kindly, and if you don't know how to brew and bake she'll soon larn you and turn you into a proper Yorkshire-woman. So will you come along of me, Sarah, m'dear?"

Sarah lifted her face and he was concerned to see tears in her eyes. "A family of my own!" she said in a low voice. "A family to love and to love me! Can you ask—can you doubt that I will come?"

"Then go and pack a few clothes," he said gently. "Happen her ladyship has a maid will help you, because I've a post-chaise waiting outside and I must be off within the hour. The lambing ain't finished yet."

Now that the departure from Chevening, so ardently longed for, had come, it was so sudden and unexpected that she could scarcely believe it.

"I must tell Lady Stroud," she said uncertainly.

"Nay, I'll tell her." He got up and gave her a gentle push toward the door. "Go you now and pack. And change that dress; 'tis too thin for traveling, is that."

She ran off and left him to explain.

"My name is Hargreaves, m'lady," he told Lady Stroud. "James Hargreaves, Sarah Wakefield's grandfather, and I've come to take her home with me to Yorkshire, ma'am."

Her ladyship sat down suddenly, unable to speak, and he sat down opposite her, his hands planted squarely on his knees. "Happen I've surprised you," he said, "but I've been uneasy in my mind ever since Sam Wakefield lost her brass. 'Now,' I said to my younger daughter Ruth, 'what are we going to do with our Sarah? Don't you reckon we oughter fetch her home to Thistlethwaite?' 'Why,' she says, 'do you think them fine folk in Kent won't want her no more?' 'No,' I says, 'I don't.' If I'm wrong, m'lady, you must forgive me—my mind is slow in working such things out—but I reckoned that with the Wakefield brass in her pocket our Sarah would be welcome in any household, however grand they might be. But when one of Lawyer Adams's young men come to see me with a letter he'd had from Sarah and it seemed she was living with you, m'lady, not at Chevening Place with Sir William and his family, I knew I was right. You have meant it kindly no doubt, but our Sarah is not going to live on charity. And that's why I'm here, to fetch her home with me today."

"But of course she must go with you," said Minnie Stroud, distressed, "if that is what she wishes to do. I am only concerned for her happiness, but I shall miss her sadly. I have grown very fond of her." She repeated this to Sarah when she came to say goodbye, her luggage consisting of a reticule, and one small portmanteau to be loaded on to the waiting chaise.

"I have left my best gowns behind," Sarah told her. "Perhaps the girls' maid Tully will like them. I shall not need them any more." She took a letter from her reticule. "This is the only letter Vincent ever wrote me—scarcely a week before our wedding. I would like you to read it after I am gone and then you may destroy it if you please. It is nothing to me now." Whenever she had felt herself to be weakening and the old affection for his family returning, she had used it to steel herself against them. "I cannot say that I am sorry to leave Kent, though I shall always remember you with warm affection, dear Lady Stroud. Please make my excuses and give my respects to all at the Place." She gave her a fleeting kiss and was gone.

Minnie Stroud, scarcely able to comprehend what had happened, watched the chaise move away briskly out of the drive, and when it had gone she went back to the drawing room to read Vincent's letter.

Sophia was angry with Sarah for having left without coming to make her goodbyes in person. She said she had behaved with great ingratitude.

"Sarah was never ungrateful in the old days," Liz said thoughtfully. "And though her manner changed lately, I think she was still fond of us. Dear Sarah. I hope she will be happy in Yorkshire."

Sophia said she hoped so too, in a tone that meant the opposite. "She must have written to her grandfather behind your aunt's back," she went on. "And if she did it was very unkind of her, besides being deceitful. I daresay she said some untrue things about us all, because I do not see any other reason why he should have come down in such a hurry to take her away from the lodge. All in the space of an hour, your aunt said."

"But Aunt Min was not angry with Sarah about it," protested Liz. "Because I asked her and she said no, her anger was all for somebody else, but she would not say who it was."

It was a puzzle to which there seemed to be no key, and Sophia's conscience was not clear enough for her to want to pursue the subject. Fortunately there were preparations to be made for her daughters' visit to London, and Sarah's behavior was soon dismissed from her mind.

In the end the Chevening traveling coach was chosen for their journey, the servants and luggage following in Lady Stroud's smaller one. The traveling coach was a very grand affair ornamented with the Chevening coat of arms, the liveries of the servants and outriders—for it was drawn by a team of six—taking up the colors of mulberry and dark green, with crested silver buttons echoing the *d'argent* in the arms.

Edward's house had been cleaned from top to bottom, the rooms had fires burning cheerfully, and dinner that evening was certainly an improvement on the one that Lady Stroud had eaten in his house the previous summer. The collection had been added to quite considerably, and he took the girls round it on the following morning while his aunt called on her sister Miranda in Grosvenor Square. After they had praised some of his new purchases and abused others, Edward took his sisters for a walk in Kensington Gardens and told them of the festivities he had planned for their entertainment. That evening they would visit the new theater in Drury Lane, where Macbeth was being played by Macready himself.

Frank and Lucinda Crayne happened to be at the theater that night with Lady Winter, and during the interval they came and spoke to the Chevenings. They had just arrived in London from Crayne Castle, and Edward was not pleased to see Mr. Dunfoyne in close attendance.

"It must be so romantic," sighed Liz, "to live in a castle."

"It is not in the least romantic," Lucinda assured her, "as Mr. Dunfoyne can tell you. He and Clara have just been visiting us at Crayne. Castles are cold and draughty and any rooms that could be made habitable are usually hung with tapestries ages old, depicting boar hunts or battle scenes or something equally gory. Isn't that so, Gerald?"

"You have forgotten to mention stone staircases and the priest's cell," he reminded her with a look that Edward deplored. "Every self-respecting castle has a priest's cell."

"Haunted?" asked Liz apprehensively.

"Invariably," said Gerald solemnly, and Lucinda laughed.

"I do not believe your uncle lives in such a place," protested Liz, and Lucinda admitted that she was right.

"My grandfather had a Gothic taste in architecture and he employed Mr. James Wyatt, who liked building houses with battlements and turrets and things of that nature, to rebuild the ruined gatehouse as a country mansion that would fit in with draughty old Crayne." It was quite beautiful, that house, with windows that looked out over the plain below the castle—a most romantic prospect as Liz would say. But it had cost so much to build that her uncle had only just finished paying for his father's extravagance that spring. They talked of the castle while Maria searched the audience eagerly to see if she could find a certain person, who turned out not to be there. As they were about to return to Lady Winter's box, she recalled her manners sufficiently to ask Lucinda if she had heard that Sarah had left them for Yorkshire.

"Oh yes," Lucinda said, smiling. "I have had a letter from her."

"A letter?" The girls were astonished.

"You are indeed honored," Edward said dryly, his dislike for Mr. Dunfoyne making him cooler than usual. "She did not write to my aunt, did she, Aunt Min?"

"I did not expect it," said his aunt quietly, and Lucinda said that it had not been a long letter. It was only to tell her that she was very happy, that she loved her grandfather and her Aunt Ruth, and that the farmhouse was beautiful.

Lucinda and her aunt went back to their box, with Mr. Dunfoyne beside them. She included Edward in her departing curtsy, which he returned with an unsmiling bow.

After the girls were in bed that night, Edward asked his aunt why she had not expected a letter from Sarah. "I should have thought she owed *you* a word or two of thanks," he said.

Lady Stroud said that she and Sarah had parted on affectionate terms. "But I am a Chevening, my dear, and there were reasons—private ones—why she wished to sever all connection with the family. I can only say that in her place I would have done the same." And with that he had to be content.

Lucinda's thoughts had also returned to Sarah, and she

wondered rather miserably, and not for the first time, if all the Chevening men were like Vincent, and if, under their charming manners and polite conversation, Edward and Jasper might not also be capable of the cruelty that their eldest brother had exhibited.

It would be a pity, she thought, to lose her heart to one of them and find out her mistake when it was too late. She determined to keep a tight rein on her feelings where Edward was concerned; she could not forget how her pulses had quickened at the sight of him that evening, and she made up her mind to avoid him during the whole of his sisters' visit. Here she was not entirely successful, Frank being his greatest friend, and as a result Mr. Dunfoyne's hopes were raised to heights that rendered him almost dizzy with delight.

The girls' Aunt Miranda, encouraged by Lady Stroud, gave a small dance for them during their visit, while Edward returned her hospitality with a musical evening. When Sir Berkeley Winter came at last to pay his promised call, however, Edward was able to suspend somewhat his duties as host and take up his cherished role as art collector.

The baronet was flatteringly envious of the little madonna.

"You think it may be a genuine Raphael?" Edward asked.

"It might be. In fact, I would like to bring somebody I know to look at it and have his opinion. He is interested in such works of art and does not think that the old masters are sufficiently appreciated by the English as a nation."

"Bring anyone you choose, sir. I shall be honored,"

said Edward. Sir Berkeley glanced at him sharply and smiled.

"Well, we shall see," he said.

The girls' stay was to last until the second week in May, and they were paying their final visit to the theater when Mr. Delamere came to their box to pay his compliments. To Lady Stroud, his effrontery seemed extraordinary. He showed none of the subdued sorrow that had so impressed Vincent's parents; in fact he might not have had even a fleeting memory of what had occurred. He was the old swaggering, conceited Rick, boasting of his horses, in particular of a race horse that had won at Newmarket and the bets he had placed on it and won.

Had they been in London long, he wanted to know? He had lately been at Eldon with his father, who was growing positively senile. "If I don't run when he sends for me he threatens to cut me out of his will," he complained with his loud laugh. "He can be a most devilishly awkward customer when he pleases."

Lady Stroud watched and listened as he talked easily with her nieces, and when Maria told him that she and Liz were to stay in Brighton with Mme. St. Clair during June, a glance passed between them that did not please her at all. Her uneasiness was not lessened when the last act began and, with bows all round, the odious young man took his leave. He expressed the hope that he would see the young ladies in Brighton in June, and promised them that he would be sure to visit his mamma there in her house on the Steine.

Ten

Nearly every morning Edward had prevailed upon his sisters to accompany him on his ride in the park before breakfast, but on the day that they were leaving he had to set out with Tod as his only companion.

He had almost completed the round of the park when Frank Crayne caught up with him. Lucinda was a lazy piece, he said; he could never rouse her for an early ride while they were in London. "Has Jasper told you of our visit to Andover?" he asked.

"You mean the fight for the championship? No, I have not seen him since he returned, and yesternight he sent word by his servant that he was in no shape for another late night, but I gathered from his man that it was a disappointing mill—only lasting five rounds."

"Yes, we had expected at least thirty. But when we were on the way back he questioned me closely about

Vincent's accident last August. Has he said anything to you about it?"

"Not a word."

"It seems that one of his brother officers happened to remark in his hearing that he would suspect anything in which Rick Delamere had a hand, and it put a doubt into his mind. He now thinks there may have been something odd about the accident, and that in fact it was no accident at all."

"Jasper enjoys making a mystery where none exists," said Edward tolerantly. "What is his notion of the business then?"

"He said that Vincent was a good and careful driver—"

"Which you know as well as I do is not true."

"Yes. But he also said that he found it hard to believe Vincent would try to overtake Delamere on so narrow a bridge. What is your opinion?"

Edward frowned. "As you said just now, Vincent was neither a good nor a careful driver, and neither is Delamere. Put them behind a pair of horses like Vincent's bays or Delamere's blacks and they would go mad, and if there was a wager in it they would be ten times worse."

"That is exactly my view of the matter," agreed Frank. "I told Jasper that Dunfoyne had been in the house party last August and he would have told me had there been anything wrong. But I don't think he believed me."

"Jasper's always putting up hares," said Edward. "Think no more of it. I know that my father questioned Vincent's groom, Hookey, about the accident and that his story tallied with Delamere's. He was far more distressed about the loss of the bays."

"Don't know that I blame him. They were beautiful animals."

"So they should have been, at the price my brother paid for them," said Edward grimly. He said he would have a word with Jasper after his sisters and aunt had gone that morning. "I shall tell him not to be a fool and to let the matter rest."

They came to the parting of the ways and Edward went back to Sloane Street and found Jasper, his handsome face all health and good humor, having breakfast with his relatives before their departure and devouring the mutton chops that Edward's cook had provided for her master with an appetite. As he ate he enlarged upon the fight at Andover.

"It was a thousand pities you were not there," he told his brother. "You would have enjoyed it above all things. Tom Spring against Bill Neat. It had been planned to take place on the Hungerford Downs and I heard yesterday that the people of Newbury had looked to making a nice penny out of it, with provisions sold, drinks, lodgings and stabling. They reckoned the county lost ten thousand pounds because of the stupidity of the magistrates in not allowing it."

"Andover was as good, I daresay." Edward helped himself to what Jasper had left of his chops.

"Oh, it was an excellent choice. The hill made a natural amphitheater and by the time we got there at eight o'clock crowds had been collecting all night and carriages and drags were still arriving. There were wagons holding as many as twenty people standing, each paying a pound apiece."

"Twenty pounds a wagon! Why, they couldn't have been worth that when they were turned out of the wheelwrights."

"That is what Frank said. And the ringside seats consisted of bales of straw that exchanged hands at ten pounds."

"I cannot understand," said Lady Stroud severely, "how gentlemen can pay such prices for the pleasure of watching a prize fight." She got up from the table. "Do not linger too long, my dears. Purchase and Tully will be finishing our packing and waiting for the portmanteaus to be strapped. We must start not later than ten o'clock."

She left the room and Maria followed her, while Liz lingered to ask if anybody had tried to stop the Andover fight.

"There was a rumor to the effect, but directly they heard of it the Duke of Beaufort, the Duke of Marlborough, and several of their friends went to see the mayor and had no difficulty in persuading him to let it continue."

"And did you win a nice lot of money?" asked Liz hopefully.

"That I did not, for I backed the wrong man." Liz laughed, and then ran off upstairs.

"A lot of us had money on Neat," Jasper told his brother, "but Spring confounded him from the start by avoiding those terrific rushes of his and countering all his heaviest punches. Added to which the poor fellow broke his arm in the last throw of the fifth round and had to toss in the sponge. Nobody can win a fight with a broken arm."

"It would make such a prospect doubtful," agreed Edward. Upon learning that the Chevening carriage was outside, Jasper went to have a word with the coachman, leaving his brother to finish his breakfast in peace.

After his guests had left, Edward went up to his gallery to place a picture—a new acquisition—in a better light.

Jasper followed him a while later, and abused the portrait heartily.

"I have seldom seen such an ugly old woman," he commented. "Yellow wrinkled face, beady black eyes, gray hair pulled back under a plain cap, and to crown it all, a black dress! What persuaded you to buy such a thing?"

"I liked it." Edward placed it opposite the windows where the light fell on it, and stepped back to study it. The white ruff round the neck of the dress looked as if it had been freshly starched, and the old lady's eyes that Jasper condemned as beady followed him across the room, twinkling as if, from her advanced years, she were amused at the whole of life. Yellow and wrinkled as she was, she was very much alive. "It is a Dutch portrait," Edward said.

"I dislike Dutch paintings—the subjects are so coarse. I hope you did not pay a great deal for it?"

"My faithful Grimble went up to four pounds and was afraid I had been robbed, but Frenchmen will pay handsomely for pictures such as this."

"Take my advice then and find a Frenchman and sell it to him at a profit. Who was the artist?"

"Franz Hals."

"Never heard of him. But I didn't come here to talk about your collection." Jasper walked restlessly to the window and stood looking down at the street below. "And I have not come to borrow money either, so you can put that out of your mind."

"My dear fellow, you know I am always happy to be your banker; the sums you need are very modest ones considering your expenses."

"You are damned good to me, Edward. But I have come to talk to you about Vincent's accident."

So that hare had not been laid yet. Edward kept silent, and Jasper went on, "Edward, I do not believe it was an accident at all. I think it may have been staged to look like one, but I think Delamere deliberately overtook Vincent on the wrong side of the road and forced him through that fence. In other words, Rick Delamere murdered our brother."

"That is a grave charge to make against a man. Have you spoken to Hookey about it?"

"I cannot speak to Hookey. He has gone."

"What do you mean? If he is not in Dover Street he will be at Chevening."

"But he isn't. When I spoke to old Weldon just now he told me Hookey had given in his notice after Vincent's death and has not been seen since."

"Does anyone know where he has gone?"

"If Weldon knew, he wouldn't tell me. But it looks as if he has bolted, and I know why. Hookey was the only witness to that accident besides Delamere and his groom, and I think he was warned to hold his tongue unless he wanted to follow his master."

"Jasper, my dear fellow, you are allowing your imagination to run away with you. I do not like Rick Delamere any more than you do, but I will not believe that he would send a friend to his death for the sake of a wager, nor that he would threaten his friend's groom to silence him."

Jasper was far from convinced by this argument, and after he had returned to his barracks Edward asked Tod if he knew Hookey's whereabouts.

Tod said he did not know anything about Hookey,

except that he had a sister who was one of the house-maids in Dover Street.

"Charlie Birch, the tall footman there, he did say as he thought Hookey might be afeared of summat and that was why he left in such a 'urry," he offered.

"Afraid? But why? Surely he did not think any of the family blamed him for the accident?"

"I don't rightly know what Birch meant, but that's what he said. But he's a great gossip, that one, and it's my belief what he don't know he makes up."

A little while before, Edward had laughed at Jasper for his suspicions, but now he, too, was growing disturbed. That afternoon he walked to Dover Street and saw the housekeeper there, Mrs. Flynn. She was an imposing lady with an air of martydom because she felt the move from St. James's Square to Dover Street had lowered her and the family.

"You want to speak to the Hookey girl, Mr. Edward? I hope she's not done anything wrong?"

"Certainly not, Mrs. Flynn. I only want to know if she can tell me where to find her brother. He was Mr. Vincent's groom."

"Oh, yes, that is why she came to London, to be near him. Very close they was, Hookey and her brother." The housekeeper left, and Matilda Hookey came to the library—a much smaller one than St. James's Square, most of the volumes having been sent to Chevening with the busts of the Roman emperors. She stood there awkwardly, bobbing a curtsy and pleating and repleating her apron with nervous fingers as she waited for him to speak, her eyes large with fright under her mob cap.

"Ah—Matilda, is it?" said Edward. She nodded speech-

lessly, bobbing again, and he went on kindly, "I understand your brother left my family's service after Mr.
Vincent's accident."

"Yes, sir."

"Do you know why?"

"He said he wasn't going into private service no more,
sir."

"I see. What is he doing now if he is no longer in
private service?"

"Please sir, he's an ostler at an inn."

"Can you tell me where?"

The apron corner was pleated and repleated more as-
siduously than before. Then, "I'm sorry, sir," burst out
Matilda, half-tearful, half-defiant. "I don't know as I can."

"Don't you know where he is?"

"Oh, yes, sir, I do, but I promised him I wouldn't say
because he don't know if he'll like 'otel work after being
private. But before he goes he says to me, 'If I likes it,
'Tilda,' he says, 'I will find you a place in the same 'otel as
chambermaid.' And I'd like that, sir, because we've allus
been mortal fond of each other, Bob and me, because
you see, we'm all we've got. But if Mrs. Flynn was to
know she'd fly in a rage and give me notice wi'out warning, sir, and then what would I do, wi'out a character nor
nothing?"

"Matilda, nobody is going to tell Mrs. Flynn anything.
I had hoped to talk to your brother about the accident
last August, but it is of no consequence. Did he ever
speak of it to you?"

"Oh yes, sir. It was them 'osses, you see, sir. When
they was killed like that it made him so mortal angry he
give his notice the next week. I never see him so angry
before. Very fond of 'osses is Bob."

The bays had indeed been far too fine to die in such a way, but it seemed that little help was to be gained from Bob Hookey or his sister. Edward thanked the girl, gave her a half-crown, and told her not to think of it any more. "If your brother don't want anybody to know where he is, why he's welcome to his secrets."

"Thank you, sir." She bobbed again and then, as she turned to the door, she said, " 'Course if you was to call in at the King's Head in Norwich . . . if you happen to be that way . . . I wouldn't say as you might not find him. And I'd be grateful to know how he's faring among all them foreigners, Mr. Edward, sir, because he ain't one for letter-writing, ain't Bob, and I'm not much of a 'and at it meself."

"I will see what I can do."

After she had gone he sat for a while thinking it out. It scarcely seemed worthwhile to travel to Norwich to see a man who cared more for the death of a pair of horses than for their owner who had broken his neck. Edward did not believe anything could come out of pursuing the matter further, and he told Jasper so when he called upon him that evening.

"I know where Hookey is," he said, "but as he does not want it to be known I am not divulging his whereabouts to you or to anybody else." His tone implied that the business was finished as far as he was concerned, but Jasper was triumphant.

"This confirms my suspicions!" he cried. "The man is in terror of his life!"

"Oh, my dear fellow, do not be so dramatical!" His elder brother was bored with his heroics. "Will nothing persuade you to let the matter drop?"

"Nothing," said Jasper firmly. "I intend to find out the

truth. Delamere has been saying it was Vincent's bad driving alone that sent him through that fence. I mean to kill that lie."

"If it is a lie," Edward said skeptically, and then, as Jasper swore at him, "Very well. I will see Hookey and question him, but if his story tallies with Delamere's will you be satisfied?"

"No," said Jasper gloomily. "But if you are, I suppose I shall have no choice." And ungraciously he took himself off.

When his brother had gone Edward sent Tod to the Bull in Aldgate to book two outside places on the first of the morning coaches to Norwich. He liked to see and smell the countryside at that time of the year.

The first coach left at five, and by half-past four the small carriage came round to take Edward and Tod to Aldgate.

"Did Mr. Tod say where they was going?" asked the cook when the groom returned.

"No, Mrs. Paddock, he did not," he said cheerfully. "Like as not Mr. Edward's after more pictures, and that might take him anywheres. There's coaches start for places all over the country from the Bull—Exeter, Oxford, York, Bristol, Norwich, Ipswich. All I knows is I'm to meet 'em at the Bull tomorrer at five in the arternoon."

"All this traveling about arter pictures," grumbled Mrs. Paddock, topping her cup of tea with a nice drop of gin. "And then comin' 'ome expecting dinner on the table, no matter when. Why can't 'e 'ave 'is dinner on the way like a Christian?"

It was market day in Norwich, and when the coach pulled in to the King's Head yard at six that evening, punctual to the minute, the streets were still thronged with farmers and their wives going home and the yard was full of carts.

Edward swung himself down, and while Tod went to engage rooms for the night, he looked about him for Hookey. He saw him almost directly, helping to persuade a pair of frisky three-year-olds into the shafts of a gentleman's carriage, and he waited until he had finished before he went to speak to him. The groom's expression changed as he saw him.

"What are you doing in Norwich, Mr. Edward?" he asked.

"I came to see you," Edward told him.

Hookey was busy for a moment, giving his attention to the horses as they moved out of the yard, and then he came back and said sullenly, "Who told you as I was here? 'Tilda, I s'pose, drat the girl."

"She did not tell me willingly, and nobody else knows, not even Tod who is here with me. Mr. Jasper has a notion that the accident last August was caused more by Mr. Delamere's bad driving than by Mr. Vincent's, and I have come to hear your account of the business, as you were there at the time."

"I can't talk to you 'ere, and not now wiv all these 'ere 'osses to see to," said Hookey roughly. After a moment he added in a quieter tone, "I can meet you somewheres arter ten tonight—my day is s'posed to be finished then."

"I'll meet you outside St. Peter's Mancroft on the corner of the market place at ten o'clock," Edward told him shortly, and went in to order his dinner and send Tod to book places for them both on the five o'clock mail to London the next morning.

The moon was up that night as Edward crossed the

market square, threading his way through the deserted booths to the great church on the corner. The doors were locked and there was no light in the lantern over the doorway, but he had not long to wait before Hookey joined him. He could see that the man was in a belligerent mood and had come to say what had been teasing him over the intervening months.

"Fust of all, Mr. Edward," he burst out, "you kin tell Mr. Jasper as that there h'accident was no more Mr. Delamere's fault than it was Mr. Vincent's. If Mr. Delamere'd been in a like sitivation Mr. Vincent would have thought nowt of pushing him through the fence. I don't 'old wi' speaking ill of the dead, specially seeing as Mr. Vincent was your brother, but time and agin we've druv them bays till they was blown, and when I've told him if he put 'em on the road agin afore they was proper rested they'd drop dead, he'd shout at me to remember he was the master. And the way he used the whip—them bays didn't need touching. I never see Sir William use his whip on his 'osses, nor you neither, not once in all the time I was groom at Edgecombe. But you wouldn't think them animals—both bays and blacks—was flesh and blood the way those young devils lashed at 'em. They raced acrost that Common like as if they was madmen, and I don't know as 'ow I lived to tell the tale. But if Mr. Jasper won't take my word for it, I dessay the genelman what see it all will say the same."

"Who was he? One of the house party?"

"No, sir. He wur a surgeon from Eldon what was riding acrost the Common to see a patient on t'other side. He come down the road at a canter to ax if he can help. Mr. Delamere was there by then—he come running back on foot and he was white as death. 'Yus, my young spark,' thinks I, 'you may well stare at what you've done.' Mr. Vincent was pinned under the kerridge not making a sound, but one of the bays was dead wi' a broken back and t'other's front leg was splintered and the poor critter was in agony. 'If so be as you 'ave a pistol handy, sir,' I tells the surgeon, 'you kin put this poor beast out of his misery.' 'That's soon done,' he says and he fetches a pistol from his saddle holster and he shoots it through the head. 'And now,' he says, 'give a hand to lift the kerridge off the young man if you please.' Mr. Delamere never lifted a finger, he just stood there as if he was a block of stone, but Brodie and me gets the kerridge lifted and Mr. Vincent was lying there with his eyes staring and Mr. Delamere squeaks out, 'Oh my Gawd, he ain't badly 'urt, is he?' The surgeon looks at him contemptuous like and kneels longside Mr. Vincent and takes his head and turns it gently, and then opens his coat and listens to his heart. Then he gets up briskly, a-dusts off of his hands, and says, 'Your friend is dead, sir. His neck is broke.' Then he climbs the bank, swings hisself back on his 'oss and goes off wi'out so much as a good day. When he was gone Mr. Delamere says, 'It weren't my fault, was it, 'Okey? Mr. Chevening was overtaking me, wasn't he?" I looks him in the face and I says, 'If you say so, Mr. Delamere, sir.' 'I do say so,' he says, his voice 'ight-pitched and shrill-like. 'And if anyone says any different he'll 'ave me to reckon with.' And he goes off to Eldon Court in his kerridge to send a wagon for Mr. Vincent's body."

"Did you think Mr. Delamere was threatening you?"

"Not him." Hookey laughed. "He knew as well as I did as it could have been him lying there wiv a broken neck, a smashed kerridge and two dead 'osses. It was because of them bays that I swore I'd never go into private service agin. Why, the coachmen what bring the stages in at the end of the Norwich run 'ud be ashamed to treat their 'osses as those young genelmen treated theirs."

Edward could believe it. The teams of horses in the modern, lightly sprung stages were as well-groomed as their drivers, and the man who had brought his stage up that day was a dandy to his fingertips. With his white, low-crowned hat, his white full-skirted coat of the finest cut, his polished boots with tops as clean as if he were setting out for a day's hunting, his striped waistcoat, snowy stock and driving gloves of the best chamois, he had been as good to look at as the handsome, well-cleaned harness and the beautiful cattle that he drove, each fresh team as glossy-coated as the last. These modern coachmen drove at speed, cornering with skill, allowing no more than three minutes for the changing of horses, and seldom drinking, except perhaps for a small glass of port at an inn where the wine was known to be good. They would not soil their gloves by touching a parcel or a piece of luggage, and so great was their fame that there were always those willing to come running to do it for them. Edward could understand Hookey's condemnation of Vincent and his friends.

"Thank you, Hookey," Edward said. "I am very much obliged to you." He parted with another half-crown, told the man to write to his sister, and was walking away when Hookey said, "When you see Mr. Jasper, sir, don't let him say or do anything as might put Mr. Delamere agin him. He's a bad-tempered gentleman and that groom of his, Brodie, is no better. Warn Mr. Jasper, sir, to let things bide."

Edward promised that he would, and when Jasper came

to see him after he returned to London he gave him
Hookey's message.

"I wish I had come with you," said Jasper fiercely.
"I'll wager I'd have got more out of him, damn him."

"I doubt it. I have had time to think it over since seeing
him," said his brother reasonably, "and I don't believe
Delamere had a notion that the fence would give way.
He wanted to crowd Vincent into it so that he would be
forced to pull up and let him by. It was the fence that
was to blame; old Delamere said it was rotten right through
and if it had been on his land it would have been mended
long ago."

Jasper damned old Delamere and his fences. "Hookey
said there was a surgeon from Eldon at the scene of the
accident?"

"Yes, but he was riding over the Common and he could
have seen very little of it." Bridle paths over commonland
in August were usually hedged in with gorse and bracken
and sloe bushes. "No doubt it was the sound of the crash
that drew his attention after he had reached the road."

"That is only conjecture. I can find the man and ask for
his story," said Jasper stubbornly. "There cannot be more
than one surgeon in Eldon. It is a small market town. I
shall go there tomorrow."

"I wish you would not. Think of what you are doing
before you embroil yourself—and others—in this." Edward remembered his mother, beginning to find some
of her old cheerfulness, and the girls' improved spirits,
and his father, trying to forget the heavy load of Vincent's
debts. "Do as Hookey said, there's a good fellow, and let
it bide."

Jasper ignored Hookey and his advice. "Eldon is not
more than ten or eleven miles from London," he said.

"And if you do not wish to accompany me I shall be quite content to go alone."

Edward told him he would go with him, and his younger brother smiled his relief. "You're a good fellow, Edward, damned if you are not. I wish I were not so short of money always, but I doubt if I shall ever be anything else. I shall have to hire a mount tomorrow—mine has gone lame."

"You can have one of mine and Tod can come with us on the cob. He'll enjoy that."

They went downstairs, having arranged that Jasper would be at the house at eight the following morning, and as they reached the library door Jasper said diffidently, "Talking of money, Edward—"

Edward laughed. "How much do you want?"

Jasper said ruefully that he had been forced to buy a new shako, his having been spoilt by a heavy downpour of rain, and that it would cost him thirty-four pounds.

Edward gave him the thirty-four pounds and told him to come in time for breakfast the next morning.

Eleven

That night Edward had been invited to the Winters' for dinner, Sir Berkeley having recently purchased an Alebert Cuyp that he wished him to see. Even if Lucinda had not been there he could not have resisted such an invitation, and directly he arrived he was taken into the large gallery where the collection was displayed. He admired the new picture and agreed with his host that no artist had managed to catch the light and skies as Cuyp had done. "It is beautiful," he said.

"Even to the peasants?" asked Lucinda demurely, at his elbow. He turned sharply to greet her. For once Mr. Dunfoyne was nowhere to be seen.

"Even to the peasants," he said. "Look at the action in that fellow playing his flute for others to dance to—and the child running with the dog—it is superb."

"If ever I have my portrait painted," said Lucinda, "I shall select an artist less true to life."

Edward regarded the young lady of fashion thoughtfully. Her dress was of lemon-colored gossamer, with short sleeves of blond quillings, and her headdress, of fine net and yellow roses, was fastened with amber. Amber beads were round her neck, and if the black lace scarf across her shoulders was meant to veil the low-cut bodice it was not doing its duty. It was of the texture of a cobweb.

"What artist will you choose?" he asked.

"Oh, Lawrence, of course! How handsome he has made the King! If he could do as much for His Majesty, what could he not do for me!"

Later on, as he gave her his arm downstairs to the dining room, she dropped her affectation in the sudden, bewildering way she had. "Edward, what is Jasper about? He cannot be serious in his intention to confront Delamere over Vincent's accident?"

"I hope not."

"But can you not prevent him from doing such things? You are the eldest son now; you should be able to control him."

"I do my best," he said with a faint smile.

"It is because he has not enough to do," she said severely, as she sat down beside him at the long table. "I have observed such things in young gentlemen who have not anything to occupy them. They become so bored that they are reduced to quarreling with their friends."

"And how do young ladies behave when they are bored?"

"Oh, we are seldom bored." Her eyes met his provocatively. "We are always employed, you see, in embroidery, and walking, and riding, and playing cribbage, and in reading novels, and in—"

"Flirting?" he suggested.

"Certainly not." As the soup was put in front of them, she changed the subject, asking if he were to accompany his sisters to Brighton.

"No. Will you and Frank be there? I understand Lord Crayne has a house on the Steine."

She hesitated, and then said that she and her brother did not visit Brighton during the summer. "We prefer it in the winter when, although the wind is cold and blustery, the people we meet are more to our taste."

"Then where do you go when you leave Manchester Square?"

"Frank has been summoned to Crayne again, poor lamb. I do believe my uncle would send for him if the housekeeper had the toothache. And when he returns I am to pay a long-promised visit to Salisbury, where one of my mother's sisters has a charming house in the Close. I am always happy to visit her. Her husband was related to the dean."

"And how will you occupy yourself? In embroidery, and walking and riding and playing cribbage with your aunt, and perhaps flirting with some wretched curate?"

"That is scarcely gallant of you, Mr. Chevening! Why should he be wretched if I flirted with him? It should make the poor man happy." But her eyes held laughter. "In fact, I think I might marry a curate. The dean would use his influence with the bishop and in no time at all he would become an archdeacon at least. I should enjoy being the wife of an archdeacon."

"You could never be an archdeacon's wife."

"And why not?"

He met her lightness with sudden gravity. "I have met few archdeacons in my life," he said, "but I don't think I have ever met one with a young and beautiful wife."

"Do my ears deceive me?" she cried. "Or have you paid me a compliment for the first time in your life?"

"I am afraid I have little aptitude for such things," he said, and applied himself to his dinner.

When the party was over she upbraided herself for her unkindness, while knowing that it was her only weapon against him. "I could not marry a Chevening," she told herself, "not even Edward. And what is more, I *will* not fall in love with him—I will *not!*" With this excellent intention settled firmly in her mind, she thought of nobody else until she fell asleep as the dawn broke across Manchester Square.

The following day was fine, and Edward and Jasper rode down to Eldon at an easy pace, followed by Tod. It was a pleasant little town with a Norman church and an excellent inn, where they found a landlord ready to direct them to the only surgeon, a gentleman by the name of Thomas Gordon. The doctor, who was weeding his garden when they arrived, heard their request and told them he could not help them.

"My brother Julius was still the surgeon here last August," he told them. "Eldon was too quiet for him, and so I bought this house from him and he moved to Clapham, where he has a thriving practice. A number of men of science live there, and some opulent merchants who travel to and from London daily, as it is only three miles from the bridges." He gave them his brother's address, and after resting their horses and refreshing themselves with a walk over the unlucky Common, they remounted and made their way back to London by way of Clapham, where they called on Dr. Julius Gordon.

Clapham was an extensive village situated on the outskirts of a parklike Common of two hundred acres, which had been carefully drained and planted with trees. The elegant villas around the Common had large pleasure-grounds, most of the owners being the prosperous merchants of whom Dr. Thomas Gordon had spoken.

Dr. Gordon's home was near the old manor house, now a boarding school for young gentlemen. He was an energetic man with a great deal of interest in scientific matters, a fact that had attracted him to Clapham. He took Edward and his brother into a small parlor reserved for interviewing his patients and listened while Jasper told him the reason for their visit.

"I remember the accident very well," he said when Jasper was done. "But I do not understand what it is that you want to know. It was a mishap caused entirely by the bad driving of both parties concerned."

"My brother was not a bad driver," said Jasper haughtily.

Dr. Gordon did not argue the point, but continued as if he had not been interrupted. "I had to visit a patient on the far side of the Common, and as the matter was not urgent and the morning was fine, I did not hurry. The gorse was in bloom and I like to savor it and the smell of the thyme that my horse crushed underfoot. I had been traveling down a bridle path in this way for a short while when I came to the top of an incline from which I could see the road that crosses the Common. The quiet of the morning was suddenly broken by a clattering of wheels and the thud of galloping hoofs and men's voices shouting. I soon saw what was going forward: a race between two young gentlemen in light curricles, a pair of horses in each, black in one and bays in the other."

In emotionless tones he described the behavior of the two young men as they mounted the Common, risking ditches, rabbit holes, molehills, anything that might have turned them over, in order to push in front. "The thought came to me, as I sat there on my steady old mount, that one or both would kill themselves before they had done. I do not know if this in your mind appears to be good driving, sir," he added with a grave look at Jasper, "but I am afraid I had no doubt that it was very bad indeed."

Jasper looked slightly abashed. "Can you tell me what happened at the bridge?" he asked in a milder tone.

The surgeon replied that the bridge was only wide enough to take one vehicle, the road approaching it narrowing and having fences on each side to protect travelers from a drop into the meadow beneath. Instead of slackening their pace as they came to it, however, the two drivers quickened up, lashing at their horses and yelling louder than ever.

"The outcome was never in doubt, but it happened so quickly that I could not tell at that distance if the bays or the blacks were in front when they reached the bridge. They appeared to collide, and the right-hand vehicle went through the fence. The other driver careered on across the bridge, but he must have stopped to look back; I could not see him because the trees on the far side hid him, and my concern was for the young fool who had gone down into the meadow. By the time I arrived, the driver of the blacks was there and appeared to be extremely frightened, stammering out that the fence must have been rotten and it was not his fault. I did not point out that a new fence of the stoutest oak could not have withstood such an impact; my trade is the curing of bodies, not consciences. Having affirmed that his friend was dead, I left him to make what arrangements he liked and rode on to see my patient."

"You did not recognize the driver of the blacks?" asked Edward.

"No. Should I have done so?"

"Does the name Delamere mean anything to you?"

"Oh, so that is who he was—I am no longer surprised by his driving."

"You had not attended to him professionally, I conclude?"

"My dear sir, the Delameres employ London doctors when they are ill—not a country surgeon." Dr. Gordon returned Edward's smile. "I was called in once to attend one of the servants at Eldon Court, and afterward entertained to a glass of wine in the housekeeper's parlor. She told me that the young man was a great plague to his father and that he had far too much money, but I did not listen overmuch. The Delameres are nothing to me."

"But it must have been Delamere who was overtaking my brother on that bridge," said Jasper with a return to his former fierceness. "And he is putting it about that it was due to Vincent's bad driving. A black lie against a dead man. Unless he takes it back I intend to give him the biggest thrashing of his life."

The surgeon's eyes rested thoughtfully on Jasper's large and well-fed frame. "I would be careful what you are at, sir," he said then. "I do not think Mr. Delamere's word would be taken seriously by his acquaintances, and I fear it was as much your brother's fault as it was his. It was a wonder they were not both killed."

As Edward stayed to thank the doctor for his help, the older man gave him a further word of warning.

"Your brother is very loyal," he said, "but this is a

case where loyalty should give way to caution. The gossip in Eldon is that Mr. Rick Delamere is not particular about the means he employs to get his ends, and that, bad friend that he is, he is a worse enemy."

This warning was given more weight that night by Tod, who told his master that Rick Delamere's man Brodie had once been a prize-fighter, but had never reached the championship because he had been one of the dirtiest fighters in the ring. He held to no rules and he would stoop to any trick to get his man on the ground and keep him there. "If Mr. Jasper rouses Mr. Delamere's temper, he'll have Brodie agin him as well, and I don't see as how he can win. They'll get him somewhen, will them two."

"Then we must hope that Mr. Jasper sees sense," said Edward with more cheerfulness than he felt, because, charming as he was, Jasper was not noted for his brains.

He turned up one morning in Edward's stableyard to ask Tod if his father still trained champions for the ring.

"Why Mr. Jasper, he's not done it fur years," said Tod.

"But supposing I found myself in need of country air and prefer that at Edgecombe to Chevening, do you think I could persuade him to get me in trim?"

"It depends who he's to match you agin," said Tod warily. "If it's to be somebody like Brodie, you don't know what you are at, sir."

"Thank you, Tod, but I know exactly what I'm at," said Jasper grimly. "And I'll be obliged if you do not mention that to Mr. Edward."

It had been arranged that Mme. St. Clair was to call for Maria and Liz on her way from Dover to Brighton. She arrived at Dover in a summer storm and made her

way to Chevening in a post-chaise over roads that were
bad and sticky after heavy rain. In spite of her journey,
however, she looked remarkably trim as she stepped from
the carriage, followed by her maid Hortense. Mme. St.
Clair had traveled in a dress of migonette green *gros de
Naples,* and her mantle was trimmed with broad fur and
lined with silk of ethereal blue, a color much favored by
her. Her little kid boots were of the same blue and her
Leghorn hat had a lace cornette under it, tied becomingly
round her face. She looked very fashionable and extremely French.

After greeting her cousin Sophia with affection and
holding out her hand to her host to kiss, which he did
with gallantry and twinkling glance at his wife, she studied
the girls critically and pronounced them to be prettier
than she had expected. "These English complexions," she
sighed. "We cannot find them in France! But it is high
time that Maria is married. Ann-Marie is only seventeen
and she is making an excellent match, entirely arranged
by myself and the parents of our future son-in-law, because my dear husband remains always in Lyons, only
concerned with the mating of his pigs!"

She laughed lightly, tapped Maria on the arm, and
said they must certainly find a husband for her, and went
away to her room to change her dress for one of geranium
red which she wore with a gold chain, an eye-glass, and a
French lace cap with bows of the same red.

At dinner she chattered on about the terrible journey
she had endured and the rudeness of the French sailors.
"I told them if it had been an English boat they would
not have behaved so. English sailors know how to behave
toward a lady."

She went on to inform them that her future son-in-law's

father had been an officer in Bonaparte's army, and the emperor had rewarded him with a château and an estate that he fancied. When Louis Phillippe returned to France, he was unable to restore the château and land to their rightful owner, who had died on the guillotine. His Majesty had no money, while the emperor's protégé was exceedingly wealthy, and his money was welcome in the royal coffers. So His Majesty had made him a comte and left him in peace with his possessions.

"The comte and his wife are delighted to have one of the old régime for their son's wife," went on Henrietta, smiling her satisfaction. "Though my poor husband had to promise a dowry of five thousand pounds for her, which is why I am in England now."

"If you have property you are hoping to sell to raise such a sum, I am afraid you may be disappointed," said Sir William, thinking sadly of the acres he had recently sold. "The country is still in a state of penury after the last war."

Henrietta looked thoughtful and said that the money might be obtained without selling any property, but she did not say how.

Before tea was brought to the drawing room, while the girls listened with amusement to Henrietta's description of the Paris fashions, Sophia studied her cousin with affection. She was a little put out, though, when Henrietta conversed with the girls in French and told them that their accents were deplorable.

"They had an excellent governess," Sophia protested.

"But an Englishwoman—that is certain!—with an English accent!" said Henrietta, laughing. "But it is of no account. I shall have friends staying with me, and one or two from Paris who will soon correct them, and there will be room in the house on the Steine for the excellent Edward. I am looking forward to welcoming Jasper there too. I understand that he has poor Vincent's looks."

And then tea was brought in, and Sir William joined them and asked about M. St. Clair. A short time later, Henrietta went to her rooms.

"I shall find Hortense there, having driven your house-keeper mad by demanding a hot fire at which to heat irons for my dresses, or else suffering from a bilious head-ache and ready to receive me with the face of a martyr. And I am tired out and will be grateful for my bed." She made her goodnights with grace, and after warning the girls not to be too late, as they would be making an early start in the morning, she left them.

"What do you think of her?" asked Sophia later when she was alone with her husband.

"She appears to be a sensible woman," said Sir William, who in fact found her too Frenchified for his liking.

"She has become *very* French," said Sophia. "But I am sure the girls will come to no harm with her, and it will give them a month of sea air."

In the morning there was a great deal of bustle to get them off, and it was not until they had been gone for at least half an hour that she remembered she had not warned Mme. St. Clair about Rick Delamere. But, as Sir William had said, she was a sensible woman, and with her French friends about her she would not have the time or inclination to look up her old friend Lady Harriet.

Twelve

In the meantime, at Edgecombe, Jasper was discovering that serious training for a fight was an entirely different matter from sparring in the inn yard at the Green Man. When he told its landlord what he was after, the ex-champion looked him up and down, told him that he had become much too fat, and the thing to do was take a course of physic and after that commence walking exercises of between ten and twelve miles a day, increasing them then to eighteen and to twenty-five. He would need to run regularly, morning and evening, a quarter of a mile at his top speed.

What with the physic and the exercise, Jasper's weight was reduced by more than three stone in a very short while. It was only then that his tutor allowed him to begin sparring again.

As old Tod's training increased in severity, Jasper's enthusiasm for it waned, but at the end of a month he returned to London in much better condition than when he had left, convinced that nothing could stop him now from thrashing Delamere once he could get him on his own.

The second morning after his return to London, he visited Sloane Street, where he found Edward in the library with the knowledgeable Grimble. He had just instructed him to bid for two pictures by George Stubbs, *Dogs in a Landscape* and *Ponies in a Landscape*, that were to be sold at Mr. Christie's sale rooms in the following week. From inquiries he had made, Mr. Grimble fancied they would cost every penny of one hundred and fifty pounds apiece, but Edward had purchased nothing since the Franz Hals and he did not think that three hundred pounds would ruin him. The pictures were small and would fit in nicely on either side of the country scene over the chimney-piece in the gallery upstairs. Having dispatched Mr. Grimble with instructions to bid for them, he greeted Jasper kindly and told him he looked much better for his stay at Edgecombe.

Jasper did not mention Delamere, and his brother hoped he had put that unpleasant young man out of his mind. He was considerably startled when Jasper told him gloomily that he had almost made up his mind to sell out of the 14th Light Dragoons.

"Surely you are not going to the Heavies?" And then, as he did not answer, Edward asked if he had spoken to his father about it.

"Not yet. The old fellow won't like it by half, but he will like it still less if I get into the hands of the moneylenders."

"Good God, no, you must not do that."

"I know I should be able to keep within the bounds of

the five hundred pounds a year that my father gives me—
many of our fellows have less than that. And I know he
gives me my mounts, and I wish they were cheaper, but
the colonel will not consider one under eighty pounds,
and replacements are sometimes more than that. How
he expects his cornets to pay for 'em out of a pay of eight
shillings a day is more than anybody can discover. But
that is not all. There is a rumor that he is to design an
entirely new uniform for his officers simply to curry favor
with His Majesty, who, as you know, has a love for uni-
forms, and the more elaborate they are, the better. A
new uniform in the Fourteenth is going to cost me at
least one hundred and fifty pounds."

He broke off, staring unhappily at the books on the
library shelves. "I do not have many debts, as you know,
Edward, but—" Again he broke off, more unhappily still.

"I conclude that there is one debt that is worrying you
more than others?" suggested his brother gently.

"It's a young woman," burst out Jasper, relieved to get
it off his mind. "The actress, Polly Porter. She is a lovely
creature but with a heart of stone. She wrote to me
while I was at Edgecombe threatening to go to my father
unless I paid her some money."

"A demanding young woman?"

"I did not think she was—in short, I was very fond of
her—but lately she is never satisfied, and she thinks all
the officers in the Fourteenth are as wealthy as Croesus."

"How much does she want?"

"Two hundred and fifty pounds."

"But that is iniquitous. You will refuse to pay it, of
course."

"I don't know if I dare. She is a remarkably determined young person."

"Can you find any part of such a sum?"

"Not a penny." Jasper's gloom deepened. "I was hoping—" He stopped short. "But I have not repaid the last fifty you loaned me yet."

"Shall we look on that fifty as a gift? I do not like loans between us. The young woman has not attempted to get you to marry her, I conclude?"

"She knew from the start there was nothing like that in the wind." Jasper gave a wry smile. "She'll look for higher game than I am when the time comes."

"If she has no legal claim on you, Mr. Brayford ought to be able to settle everything without much difficulty." He smiled encouragingly at his brother. "I will write a letter to him at once instructing him to pay Mrs. Porter the money she is demanding, and you may take it to him yourself."

After Jasper had left with the letter in his pocket, Edward wrote a second letter to young Mr. Grimble, telling him that circumstances did not permit him to buy the Stubbs pictures they had discussed that morning. He felt nothing but relief that Jasper still came to him to solve his problems instead of going to his father. Sir William would be only too ready to think that Jasper was following in Vincent's footsteps, and there he would be wrong. Much as Jasper had admired and defended his eldest brother, his own follies were only those of youth, and in a regiment where young officers gambled away thousands of pounds in a night to alleviate their boredom, he had kept free from large debts in a way that told of sacrifice of pride as well as an awareness of his duty to his family that had been completely lacking in the profligate Vincent.

Later that day, however, Edward received a letter

from Sir Berkeley Winter that put Jasper's troubles out of his mind completely. He was forced to read it again and then to indulge in a rare glass of brandy. It took him a little while to compose a reply, and after his groom had been dispatched with his answer, he summoned Tod and sent him to engage a post-chaise from the nearest livery stables.

"I must leave for Chevening at once," he told him, "and we must travel post all the way."

"You are going to the Place, sir?" Tod was accustomed to his master's sudden journeys. "To fetch something for the collection?"

"We are fetching something," Edward said. "Or rather, I hope to be fetching somebody—and we are not going to the Place."

After an hour and a half's run he arrived at Chevening Lodge in time for dinner with his aunt. She greeted him with pleasure and told him that by great good fortune she had his favorite dinner of roast duck and freshly picked peas. Then she asked him if he were staying at the Place.

"No," he said. "I am staying here tonight if you will have me, Aunt Min."

"Why of course." She appeared so mystified, however, that he did not long delay in enlightening her.

"I do not want my mother and father to know any-thing about this visit to you," he said. "I had a letter from Sir Berkeley this morning. It seems that he has mentioned my modest collection to—a certain ele-vated personage—and the gentleman in question has expressed a desire to see it for himself, strictly incognito, when he is in London tomorrow se'enight."

"My dearest Edward!" His aunt could scarcely believe it. "This is an overwhelming honor. And you have not told your parents?"

"No, ma'am." He made a small grimace. "The truth is that I need a hostess for the occasion, Aunt Min, and even if Mamma would consent to perform that duty for me, it would look odd if my father did not accompany her. And as it is not a matter of this . . . elevated personage having expressed any wish to meet my relatives, it might make a pother of it. Naturally, the gentleman will bring his own friends—Sir Berkeley tells me there may be twenty or thirty who will accompany him—and in that number there will no doubt be ladies. I must therefore have a lady in my house to help me to entertain them. Aunt Min, you are accustomed to such society—will you be my hostess?"

Only for a moment did she hesitate, before she nodded and said, with sparkling eyes, "I shall get into a fine scrape at the Place when they hear of it, but I am extremely honored that you should ask me, and I will do my best not to disgrace you, Edward. It will need a certain amount of thought, and as your guest is expected tomorrow se'enight, it would be wise for me to arrive next Monday. I will bring with me my cook and two of the upper maids, besides Purchase. Supper can be offered in that little ante-room behind the Collection. Such refined refreshments as will be required are far beyond the powers of *your* cook, Mrs. Paddock. Send her off on board wages for a week from next Monday. Your two little maids can help my cook in the kitchen and I will bring my young footman. Tod will do very well to open the door to your guests; he has grown so like his father that I should not be surprised if His—

I mean, your elevated guest—does not think he has stepped back ten years or more when he sees him. The Prince Regent was a great patron of the ring, was he not?"

"Bless you forever!" Edward gave his aunt a hug that knocked her cap awry. "I should have been completely overthrown without you. But you talked of my parents finding out; they must not find out. The whole visit is to be kept secret."

"But I suppose the Conynghams will accompany the . . . elevated personage," she reminded him smiling. "It will soon leak out."

"But not through you or me or any of our servants, please." Edward spoke in the tone Sir William sometimes used when he expected an order to be obeyed, and Lady Stroud hid a smile.

"I will be as silent as the grave, my dear," she said, and then they went into the dining room arm-in-arm to eat the duck and peas.

Edward returned the following day to London, and on Monday his aunt arrived, bringing with her a retinue of servants, a fine crimson satin dress and all her jewels.

Sir William and Lady Chevening were surprised to hear that she had left for London without taking leave of them first. "I suppose she has gone to visit Miranda," Sophia said, put out. "Nobody appears to know where else she could have gone, and I take it very remiss of her not to tell me she was going. She never visits London without coming here to discover if I have any errands for her to execute while she is there. And she was here on Sunday and never said a word." Sir William admitted that it was odd.

Two days later, he had an unexpected visitor at Chevening Place. Since he had taken up residence at the Place, certain judicial duties had fallen to his share, and he received the young woman who was shown into the justice room there without any great surprise. It was unusual for a lady to come alone in a post-chaise to see him, but it had been done before, and he was ready to receive all those who came to him for assistance or advice.

The woman's air of familiarity annoyed him, however; he was accustomed to a more deferential approach.

"You are Sir William Chevening?" she asked, sweeping him a curtsy that was as exaggerated as her manner. The thought crossed his mind that she might be an actress. He bowed and waited for her to state her business.

She looked about her at the room with an impudent smile. "Nice place you have here," she remarked. "And plenty of money too, I'll be bound."

He stiffened. "Kindly tell me what you want, madam," he said coldly.

"Certainly I will. That's what I've come for to do." She laughed, quite unabashed by his manner. "My name is Mrs. Polly Porter, and though it may mean nothing to you, it means a great deal to the young bloods what come looking for me round the stage door when the theater is closing."

So he had guessed correctly. As he still remained silent, she went on, a shade more defiantly. "I told Mr. Jasper Chevening, I warned him from the start. 'If you want to put an end to our acquaintance,' I said, 'you'll have to pay for it. I'm not a rich man's toy,' I said, 'to be taken up and put down when he thinks fit. Two hundred and fifty pounds is my price, Cornet Chevening,' I said, 'and not a penny less or I'll go to your father.' 'For God's sake don't do that, Polly,' he says. 'I'll go to my brother what has helped me before,' he says. 'He'll sell some of the pictures what he's always buying, and he'll pay you the money. Just wait a day or two,' he says, 'and you shall have it.' So I waited—more'n a day or two, more like a week or two, and he didn't come near nor by. So I went to his quarters and they told me as Cornet Chevening was in the country at Edgecombe Manor near Bath. So I went to see his high and mighty brother in Sloane Street and I got the same answer there—Mr. Edward Chevening was out of town. So then I sat down and wrote to Jasper, reminding him that I had promised to go to his father and that was what I was going to do, and when I got no answer to that I said to meself, 'My girl,' I said, 'you're on a losing horse.' And so here I am, and I want that two hundred and fifty pounds, if you please, Sir William. I'm not leaving this grand house of yours without it."

The sum she demanded was preposterous, but at the same time Sir William did not wish to have trouble with the woman. Better to get rid of her before Sophia found out; Jasper was her darling now that Vincent was gone.

He sat down at the table and said abruptly, "I cannot believe that my son is the only one to enjoy your favors, but I will give you fifty pounds, and in return you will sign a paper promising that you will in no way molest my son and or make further demands on him or on his brother, and that all his debts to you are settled in full."

"Fifty pounds!" She laughed. "I'm not going to accept that."

"You will be wise to do so," he told her quietly. "Otherwise I shall have you taken to Maidstone and put into the gaol there for demanding money with threats."

"And who will charge me?" She tried to be defiant, but her self-assurance was ebbing.

"I will," he said. "Evidently my son omitted to inform you that besides being his father I am a magistrate and justice of the peace."

"Oh!" Her manner changed abruptly. "Beg Your Honor's pardon, I'm sure. But a girl has to look after herself, as you will be the first to allow, seeing you're a magistrate. And young bloods like your son, nice boy as he is, seem to think an actress is fair game. You can write out a paper if you like and I'll sign it. My mother was respectable—a dressmaker she was—but my father drank and she lost her employment because of it. But she had me learned to read and write, and she told me to keep off the streets, which I've done all my life. I went on the boards when I was ten years old and though I'm not a Mrs. Siddons and never could be, I can act. I'm playing Lady Macbeth at the theater in Tunbridge Wells at this moment."

"I should have thought you would have done better in comedy," he said, writing out the paper.

"Oh, but I do—I mean I have. I played Lady Teazle in *The School for Scandal* at a London theater last autumn, and I've been Viola in *Twelfth Night*." She signed where he indicated, and he opened a drawer, took out fifty sovereigns, and counted them into her hand.

"And now take yourself back to Tunbridge Wells," he said, with more sternness than he felt. "And if you promise not to worry me any more, I might bring my wife to see you act one night."

"Oh, thank you, sir." She dropped him a curtsy

that was even more sweeping than the first and put the money away into a pocket in her petticoat, showing a shapely leg as she did so. She was, he thought, a taking piece.

"Surely," he said, "there are wealthier young men than my son Jasper to pay your debts?"

"Oh, there are, sir, but they ain't like Jasper. They promise everything and do nothing. 'I'll pay your rent, Polly, my pretty dear,' they say, 'pon my soul I will.' And six months goes by and my landlady threatens to throw me on the streets. I was sorry I wrote to Jasper like I did, but I was desperate, and then the very next day I met Toby Dillon and he asked me to play Lady Macbeth down in Tunbridge Wells. I was so pleased I forgot all about Jasper, until somebody said as Chevening Place was no more'n a few miles off, and so I hired a chaise and I came to see—" She broke off, looking rather ashamed.

"To see if you could persuade me to pay out some money?" he finished for her.

"Yes, sir. But I really didn't mean to do Jasper no harm."

"And you have done him none."

As her chaise drove off, passing Sophia's little carriage on the way, his mind went back to the days when he was Jasper's age and a pretty actress was easily won, if you had the money to pay for your pleasures. He wondered where those pretty young women were now, and what had happened to them, and if some of them had eventually come to the streets. He was still thinking about them when Sophia came to find him in the justice room.

"We appear to have had a visitor," she said.

"Yes. A woman came to see me in the way of business."

His eyes did not meet hers. "Did you find Lady Moresby at home?"

"No, but the drive was pleasant." She came to him and put her hand on his arm. "Did she come to see you about—either of our sons?" she asked.

"What makes you think she did, my dear?"

"Because from the glimpse I had of her she looked to be that kind of woman."

He covered her hand with his. "Your eyes are too sharp, my love." After a moment he added, "Jasper owed her a debt, which I have settled, and there is no more to be said."

"Jasper?" She shook her head, but she was not unduly shocked. "Foolish boy. Is she an actress?"

"Yes. She is playing at the theater in Tunbridge Wells. But what concerns me most is that according to her, Edward is in the habit of paying Jasper's debts."

"Well, he is his elder brother," said Sophia indulgently. "You give him more than Jasper and he does not need it as much. You know you have only to give Edward a picture or a statue for his collection and he behaves as if he has come into a fortune!" She dismissed her second son with a laugh.

"Nevertheless I think I will go to London tomorrow to see Edward and discover exactly how much he has loaned that young rascal lately."

Sir William started out for London in the afternoon, arriving in Dover Street soon after five. After he had dined, he walked across the park in the cool of the June evening to call on his son.

Thirteen

To Sir William's surprise, the house in Sloane Street was not as quiet as usual. In the gathering dusk he could see a row of imposing carriages stretching between the street lamps, the lantern over Edward's steps shedding a special glow on the largest of them. He thought his eyes had tricked him into seeing the red and gold of royal livery among the servants there. As he mounted the steps and applied himself to the lion's head with some force, he concluded that the carriages belonged to those friends of whom Liz had spoken with so much enthusiasm.

Tod opened the door to him, and for a moment did not seem to know what to do, making no attempt to stand aside to allow him to enter.

"Mr. Edward is at home, I conclude, Tod?" said the baronet ironically, with a nod toward the carriages in the street.

"Well, he is, sir, and in a way he ain't." Tod was

flustered and put out. "We'm got exalted company here tonight, Sir Willum, but if you be so good as to step into the lib'ry I'll tell Mr. Edward as you are here."

Sir William was outraged. This was what came of encouraging Edward in his absurd collection. The young man's head had been so turned by the attention given him by Winter and his friends that he fancied himself unapproachable, even to his own father. As for this clown who acted as his footman, it was time he went back into proper service and learned respect for his betters.

"Take my card to your master at once," he said curtly, and stalked into the library where sconces of candles and a chandelier gave an almost brilliant illumination to the small apartment. He had only to wait a few minutes before Tod returned, followed by Lady Stroud.

"Minnie!" Her brother greeted her in astonishment. "So this is where you slipped off to last Monday!"

"Yes, Will. You see, dearest Edward needed a hostess for tonight and he asked me if I would come. I said I would, and I brought my cook and some of my servants, and I think it is all very much appreciated upstairs. There is such a nice back drawing room where a cold collation has been set out for the guests." She paused. "May I take a message to Edward?"

"Thank you, but I will see him myself."

"Oh no, Will dear. I am sorry, but you cannot do that." As she moved between him and the door he noticed for the first time that she was wearing her best ball gown of crimson satin, and with it all her most valuable jewelry, the diamonds in her hair flashing in the candlelight.

"Edward is entertaining somebody of great importance—a most elevated personage who has come particularly to see his collection and the Raphael, having heard of it through Sir Berkeley Winter." She fixed her eyes anxiously on her brother's face. "So please may I give Edward a message, Will, dear?"

For a moment he hesitated, and then his mind turned to the carriages outside and to one in particular, with red and gold liveries. There had been a carriage next to it with a coat of arms that had also been familiar—that of the Conynghams. And as he realized who Edward's visitors were, he remembered how he had thought of his son a few moments before, and a sense of shame made him angrier still.

"Very well," he said shortly. "Tell him to come and see me in Dover Street tomorrow morning. I shall wait in for him." And he walked stiffly out into the hall. There, while waiting for Tod to open the door, he heard a voice in the saloon upstairs say, "Nollekens, hey? And from Chevening, you said?" There followed a laugh, and then the words, "My dear boy, what a cobbler that fellow was! As fine a cobbler as ever lived, I'd say, would not you, Mr. Chevening?"

There was an easiness about Edward when he called on his father the next morning, an air of amusement and an unaccustomed command of the situation that surprised his father. The excuses he had expected were of the briefest description.

"I must apologize for not being able to receive you last night, sir," Edward said. "But a friend had told His Majesty of my unimportant collection, and I had a letter last Monday se'night telling me that the King would like to see it and would call upon me yesterday evening, but that his visit was to be kept strictly incognito. His Majesty brought his own friends, but, as is usual in these cases, I was not expected to ask anybody to meet him. As there were to be ladies in the party I asked Aunt Min to be my hostess—a part that she played to perfection, I may add. His Majesty was quite impressed."

Sir William was not equally impressed. "May I ask why you did not ask your mother to have the honor of entertaining so exalted a guest?" he asked.

"I did not think she would consent," Edward said simply. "And as she has never been inside my house she is not as familiar with it as Aunt Min." It was a perfectly plausible explanation, but his father did not think Sophia would like it. He changed the subject abruptly.

"I came to see you about Jasper," he said. "I wish to know to what extent you have been paying his debts and for how long."

Edward's eyebrows went up. "May I ask who told you that I had paid any of them, sir?"

"A young woman who came to see me at Chevening two days ago. She said that Jasper told her he would go to you for the money he owed her and that you would sell a picture or two to oblige him, or some such story."

"Mrs. Porter?" Edward took it calmly. He walked to the window overlooking the street and stood there staring out, his hands deep in his pockets. "I did not think she would have the impudence to go down to Chevening."

"She is acting in the theater in Tunbridge Wells."

"Ah, then that was why Brayford did not find her. I had asked him to pay her what she asked, but evidently she had already left London." He paused, and his father asked curiously: "Have you been selling your collection to pay your brother's debts?"

"Oh no!" Edward laughed. "I may have refrained from adding to it from time to time, but it is of no consequence." He turned back from the window. "Jasper is a good fellow, sir. Indeed he has been doing his utmost to keep out of debt, and those he has brought me to settle for him have been very small. I have been able to pay them with no trouble, and I am happy to do it, though I'll admit I do read him a lecture now and then, which he takes in good part. We both feel it is better for him to keep clear of money-lenders."

"Money-lenders! I hope he will never go to any of that fraternity. Why in God's name did he not come to me?"

"He did not like to, sir, after your recent experience with Vincent. I do not know what is in his mind now, but I am afraid the officers in his regiment are too wealthy for him to be able to live with them on terms of equality for much longer."

"If he sells out, what will he do?" asked Jasper's father. "I cannot see him settling down at Chevening."

Edward could not either. "The truth is that he has an adventurous spirit," he said. "And an army life in peace-time is not so much an adventure as a steeplechase."

"He should marry and settle down," said Sir William peevishly. "I will give him time to cool his heels and then I will have it out with him. Is it any use to ask what you have paid out for your brother since you have been in Sloane Street?"

Edward said he had not kept an account of those sums and that, in any case, they were trifling amounts.

Somewhat mollified, the baronet said, "I heard your august visitor last evening saying something about Nollekens being a good cobbler. May I ask what he meant?"

"Oh!" Edward laughed, slightly embarrassed. "Years ago Nollekens used to bring back fragments of statues from

Rome every time he visited that city. He assembled the fragments into whole figures and gave them names like Zeus or Hermes or some such god or goddess. They were cemented together very carefully, in a way peculiar to himself, and stained with tobacco-water to give them an antique finish. When he had done, nobody could have told them from genuine antiques from Rome. As a sculptor in his own right, though, he is going downhill fast. His Majesty thinks he will not last much longer."

"And the Hermes is one of his put-together pieces?"

"I am afraid so, sir." After a moment, Edward added enthusiastically, "His Majesty thinks my Raphael is genuine. Sir Berkeley wished him to see it; he said that if His Majesty said it was a Raphael I could be almost sure that it was."

Sir William came to his son and rested his hand on his shoulder affectionately. "You're a clever fellow, Edward," he said. "I wish I had half your brains. You must get them from your mother, for you never had them from me."

After Edward had gone, Sir William sent word to Mr. Brayford that he would like to see the young clerk who acted as Mr. Edward Chevening's agent in purchasing pictures. When Mr. Grimble arrived, he asked him if he knew of any pictures in the sale rooms in London that his son wished to buy.

Mr. Grimble did not have to give the matter more than a second's thought. "Why yes, sir, there were those two by George Stubbs," he told him. "They were in the late Lady Westgate's sale and the price for them was one hundred and fifty pounds each, but Mr. Edward is fond of the artist's work, and they were attractive pictures. He had decided to buy them when—" He broke off abruptly. "Circumstances forced him to change his mind."

Sir William did not inquire into the circumstances. "What happened to the pictures? To whom were they sold?"

"They were withdrawn, sir, because the price offered was too small. They are coming up again in Mr. Christie's great room next week. That's on the south side of Pall Mall, sir, next to Schomberg House."

"I thought Mr. Christie had planned to move his rooms?"

"Not until the autumn, sir, when he is going to King Street. He is still in Pall Mall."

"Then go and buy those pictures. I am not particular as to price, and if you should obtain them for me have them sent to Sloane Street."

"Thank you, sir." Mr. Grimble was as full of gratitude as if the pictures had been intended for himself, and in due course they arrived in Sloane Street with a note to say that they came with Sir William's compliments and thanks.

Lady Chevening did not lightly forgive her sister-in-law for the part she had played in entertaining Edward's august visitor. "It was most deceitful of Min," she told her husband. "I cannot think why Edward did not ask me to be his hostess."

"I can think of several reasons why he did not, my dear," said Sir William in a dry tone that made her flush. "For one thing, you have never set foot inside his house, I believe."

Sophia said a bit lamely that it had never been convenient when she was in London.

It seemed to Edward, however, that his family had made a pact not to leave him in peace. Scarcely had he sent off a note of thanks to his father for the pictures than a letter arrived by express from Liz in Brighton.

"*Please, dearest Edward,*" she wrote, "*will you come to see me as soon as you receive this? They are all going to the races the day after tomorrow and plan to be out all day, but I shall not go. I do not want Mme. St. Clair or Maria to know that I have written to you, and I dare not write to Mamma because it would bring her here like a Fury and she would quarrel with her cousin and that would be more than I could endure. When I spoke to Maria about it she said I was a simpleton but I think she is besotted. I am convinced we should leave this house before HE arrives next week. Dearest Edward, please come and take us home. Your loving and distracted Liz.*"

"Now what the devil am I to make of that?" Edward tried in vain to read some sense into his sister's letter. Was it homesickness that had stricken her, or jealousy of some conquest of Maria's that made her appeal to him in this distraught fashion? Was there something more serious in the wind? It was clear that he must travel to Brighton and find out.

"This is an opportunity for using the closed carriage," Edward told Tod. It was too highly ornamented for his taste, but there were times when the sight of the Chevening arms might be welcome.

He started off the next morning, arriving in Brighton at four in the afternoon. The house on the Steine was a large one, but sparsely furnished, and the powdered footman who opened the door informed him condescendingly that only Miss Elizabeth Chevening was at home. Edward said that she was the lady he had come to see, whereupon the footman showed him into a small breakfast room where Liz was bent over some needlework. She dropped it to the floor when she saw him and fled into his arms.

"Oh Edward, my dearest brother!" she cried incoherently. "I am so thankful you have come." He could feel her trembling when he lifted her face to look at her.

"What in God's name is the matter?" he asked, and then she burst into tears. "Take hold of yourself, Liz, my dear. Go and get your bonnet and we will walk a little way along the Parade. You shall tell me everything as we go."

She ran off and soon returned with her bonnet on and a lace mantle round her shoulders. As they made their way to the Parade, the fresh saltiness of the sea air revived her.

"It started with those French friends of Cousin Henrietta's," she began. "I think they must be some of the new aristocrats she is always talking of; there is a M. Duval, and two ladies who appeared to think that because our accents were bad we did not understand the French language. Soon after we arrived they began laughing at our dresses and said that our hats were *très comique*. Maria did not give a fig for them; *she* had come to Brighton with only one purpose in mind. But one day I could not endure any more and I said, 'Mesdames, our dresses and our hats may give you a great deal of amusement, but at least nobody can say that we are mutton dressed as lamb!' They pretended not to know what I meant, but that evening Cousin Henrietta came to my room and accused me of having been impolite to her friends. 'Those two ladies that you grossly insulted,' she said, 'are noticed everywhere in Paris for their dress.' I said I was not surprised, they would be stared at anywhere in England too. Before she could fetch her breath I said that it was a pity their complexions were so yellow as it made the wearing of their white bonnets dreadfully unlucky. She went scarlet with fury and asked how I dared to criticize her guests. I said meekly, 'Cousin Henrietta, there is one thing that puzzles me about your friends. Is M. Duval *your* friend—or your husband's?' If looks could kill I should have dropped dead on the spot, but instead she whirled out of the room, for which I was very thankful. Our behavior to each other has been on the cool side since."

Edward was not surprised. "You said just now that Maria had only one object in coming to Brighton," he said. "Will you tell me what that was?"

"It was to see Rick Delamere again," said Liz. "From the first morning we arrived he has taken her out driving every day in his carriage—the same carriage, Edward, that he was using when—when—"

"When Vincent was killed. I know the one. Did Maria ever object on that score?"

"Not once. I think that love must make her lose all sense of feeling."

"Perhaps it does. Are these morning drives the only occasions when she meets him?"

"Oh no. At all the evening parties and balls he is bound to be there, and he has singled her out for attention, while she has eyes for nobody else."

"And is it that that is worrying you, Liz? That and the extremely uncivil behavior of the French ladies?"

"Oh no. Maria is old enough to realize the gossip she is attracting in the town, and the French ladies are no worse than some of Cousin Henrietta's English guests." Liz drew a deep breath. "The evening before I wrote to you we were going to a ball at Lady Harriet's, and when I was ready I found a slit in the trimming to my dress. Tully was busy with Maria's hair and Hortense likes us to know that she is Madame's maid and a very important person. So I went to the housekeeper to discover if she had some fine thread I could use to mend it. She offered to do it for me, and as she stitched it up she asked if Maria was my only sister. I said yes, and that we had had three brothers, but the eldest had been killed in a driving accident last August. She said she remembered his lordship speaking of it and saying that it was a terrible thing to have happened. I asked who his lordship was, and she replied in a surprised voice that she had been speaking of her master, Lord Crayne.

"Edward, you are at liberty to think me very stupid, but it was only then that I understood all the things that had puzzled me since we came to Brighton—the grandeur of the house, so large and splendid and yet so sparsely furnished, with things that look as if they had been brought into the light of day from dusty storerooms. The servants have an air of familiarity bordering on insolence, and except for one new barouche landau, the carriages are old-fashioned and shabby.

"I told the housekeeper, as composedly as I could, that I had forgotten we were in Lord Crayne's house and I hoped we were not incommoding his lordship with our visit. She replied that he did not plan to be in Brighton until next week. 'He will welcome you, miss, and your sister, I'm sure,' she said in a meaning sort of way, as if she were not quite as certain about Cousin Henrietta's other guests. I could guess only too well what she meant. The English ladies here have titles and beautiful clothes and jewels, and the Englishmen are full of compliments which they do not mean, but the older ones are—" She stopped, embarrassed.

"Lecherous?" suggested her brother.

"I suppose that is the word. The Frenchman, M. Duval, is much too familiar with Cousin Henrietta: he behaves in fact as if *he* owns the house and not Lord Crayne."

"And these people are all at the races today with Maria?"

"And Rick Delamere."

"H'm. Have you spoken to Maria about it?"

"Yes. I asked her if she thought Lord Crayne was Cousin Henrietta's lover and she said she had guessed it long before, that everyone had known about it for years."

"Except his own family, it seems."

"I suppose," Liz said sorrowfully, "that is why Lucinda says the air here does not agree with her or Frank in the summer months. Edward, what shall we do? My father would not allow us to stay here openly like this with Cousin Henrietta, and Mamma would never approve of her friends. I have not heard of any of them, fine as they are, being invited to St. James's Square."

"No." He gave the hand in his arm a comforting squeeze. "Leave it to me, my dear. I will get you both home before his lordship arrives—possibly tomorrow."

"Oh, thank you, Edward. I knew I could trust you."

They walked back to the Steine, arriving soon after Mme. St. Clair's house party returned from their day at the races. Henrietta greeted Edward effusively, said it was charming of him to call on her, and asked if he was staying in Brighton.

"At the Castle Inn, ma'am, for one night. I found Liz here with a headache so I took her for a walk."

"You are a good doctor, it seems." Henrietta introduced him to her guests, and as he heard the names of some of the English ladies and remembered gossip he had heard about them, and acknowledged the bows of the gentlemen, whose reputations were not unknown to him either, his sense of propriety told him that his sisters should not stay there another day.

"Will you not allow me to send a servant to fetch your luggage?" asked Henrietta. "There are plenty of rooms here."

"I am sure there are, just as I am certain of Lord Crayne's hospitality, but I am afraid I must abide by my decision to stay at the castle."

There was a sudden silence and then Duval said, "You are acquainted with Lord Crayne, sir?"

"I am, sir. His nephew Frank is my best friend," Edward told him pleasantly. Duval said he thought he should change his clothes to be ready for dinner.

Henrietta explained that they were dining early because they were going to the ball at the castle at nine o'clock. Her other guests, after curious glances at Edward, left Mme. St. Claire alone with him.

"Your visit to Brighton is quite unexpected," she said, but rather less effusively than before.

"It is a habit I have, I fear, of doing unexpected things, ma'am. For instance, I propose, now that I am here, to save my father's horses by taking my sisters back to Chevening with me tomorrow at noon." The look that passed between them was bland on his side and resentful on hers. But because of what she hoped to gain from his family she tried not to show any vexation.

"I think Liz will be glad to go," she said. "She is a spiritless little thing, and although one must recollect her youth, her manners have none of the polish that one expects in the polite world."

"I must apologize then, ma'am; Liz has always been a singularly honest child."

"You have your father's ways," she said, still trying not to reveal her anger. In Paris she had made no secret of the fact that Vincent had been her favorite. She continued with a smooth effrontery that astonished him. "Your father is a very wealthy man, Edward. One has only to visit Chevening Place to see that. I feel sure that with your assistance I can depend on him for a sum toward Ann-Marie's dowry. For your mamma's sake—because she has always been such an affectionate cousin to me."

"I am afraid that you cannot count on a great deal in that direction, ma'am. I am sure my father will wish to return your hospitality to my sisters here in Brighton and to myself and Vincent in Paris with some small token of his gratitude, but a few hundreds will be the most you can expect. The Chevening estates have been much impoverished of late, and to raise anything at all for Ann-Marie may well be beyond his powers. But you may depend on it that I will discuss the matter with him."

She was quite evidently angered by his response. "I think you are making a mistake to remove Maria," she told him. "In fact, you may very well destroy the chance of an excellent marriage for her."

"If you are referring to Delamere, ma'am, there is no chance of a marriage for Maria there."

"Why? Is he a young man of whom your father does not approve?"

"It does not greatly matter if my father approves or not," he told her. "The gossip is that Rick Delamere is married already and has been for years, and that is why his flirtations go no further than the lady concerned is willing that they should."

"Does Maria know this?"

"She may. She is not the first to be infatuated with him, and she will not be the last. Maria must learn from her mistakes."

"You sound very heartless."

"I am not so much heartless, ma'am, as within a cleft stick. What with Jasper swearing he will thrash Rick Delamere and Maria falling in love with the fellow, one can only hope that my younger brother will not visit Brighton before I take her home tomorrow."

"But he is arriving tonight, in time for dinner with us, before he accompanies us to the castle ball!" she exclaimed. "He is to stay at the Ship Inn and Rick is to meet us in the assembly rooms at the castle. *Mon Dieu*—" And she went off into a flood of French that he did not follow at all.

"It is as well then that I shall be there myself," he consoled her. When he arrived at the castle, however, a thought occurred to him, and he summoned Tod to his room.

"Tod," he said, "does your father still train men for the ring these days?" Then, as his servant hesitated, "Come, I want the truth. Did Mr. Jasper go to Edgecombe simply to have lessons in the Fancy?"

"I am sorry, Mr. Edward," said Tod, shamefaced, "but I am much afeared that he did."

Fourteen

Liz pleaded a return of her headache as an excuse not to accompany the party to the castle ball, and she told Maria that nothing would shake her decision not to attend another ball under the protection of Cousin Henrietta.

"You are exceptionally stupid," Maria said with a toss of her head. "And as for Edward taking us back to Chevening tomorrow, I suppose because he is now the eldest son he imagines he can dictate to his sisters and they will do as they are told. You may go with him if you like, but it is for me to decide when I shall leave Brighton."

Jasper arrived late for dinner. "Had to come by mail," he apologized. "When we changed horses for the last time I looked at my watch and I knew I would be late. A thousand pardons, Cousin Henrietta, but I do not object to cold soup and fish in the least, so do not put yourself out to have it warmed for me. I will change at once so that I shall not keep you waiting for your ball."

He kissed his sisters carelessly, told Liz that her headache must be due to too many parties, and left, to return later as splendid as ever in his uniform.

The house seemed very quiet to Liz after they had gone off to the ball. As she sat alone in the small drawing room overlooking the garden, the stillness was suddenly broken by a stir in the hall below. She heard a man's voice asking for Mme. St. Clair and then footsteps mounting the stairs.

The gentleman who entered the room was a complete stranger to her, but he appeared to be so much at his ease that she knew at once who he was, and dropped a curtsy in some confusion, wishing Edward were there.

"You," he said puzzled, "are not Ann-Marie?"

"No." She smiled at him timidly. "She is Cousin Henrietta's daughter. I am Liz Chevening, sir, and you must be Lord Crayne?"

He bowed. He was a tall man, fashionably dressed, with a blue swallow-tailed coat, light trousers, and the ruffled shirt, tall collar and exquisitely tied cravat of the dandy. His attire surprised her a little, because his thick hair was graying and her father, who was his age, always wore the good broadcloth of a country gentleman in town as well as at Chevening, keeping what he called the nonsense of swallow-tailed coats for smart evening entertainment.

The eyes that studied her, however, were shrewd in the extreme. "I know your brother Edward very well," he said pleasantly, "and I have met your sister Maria in London. I understood that Mme. St. Clair had invited two young relatives to stay with her here for the sake of the sea air, but she did not tell me their names."

"I do not think Mme. St. Clair expected you to arrive so soon or we should not have stayed so long," Liz said a trifle awkwardly. "Edward is taking us home tomorrow."

"Is Edward staying here with you?"

"No. He has a room at the castle for tonight. There is to be a ball there and Cousin Henrietta and Jasper, my younger brother, and Maria have gone to it with the rest of her house party, but I had a headache."

"Ladies find headaches remarkably convenient at times." He glanced at the table set out with the tea tray. "I see you have finished tea. Do you object if the servants bring me something to eat? I have not dined today."

"They shall bring it immediately." In Henrietta's absence Liz took command with an old-fashioned air that amused the man watching her, and when the footman appeared—not nearly so condescending now—in answer to her pull on the bell-rope, she told him to tell Mrs. Brenner to have dinner sent to his lordship at once.

"Will your lordship dine in the dining room?" asked the servant.

Lord Crayne glanced at Liz. "Have you any objection if I dine here at this small table?" he asked.

She had no objection at all, so the tea tray was removed, and in a very short while he sat down to his dinner at the Pembroke table with Liz opposite him, seeing that he had all he wanted to eat and wine to drink. She had the odd feeling that she had known him all her life.

"You mentioned a house party," he said as he applied himself to his meal. "I did not know that others besides yourselves were staying here."

"Oh yes." She counted them up. "Apart from my sister and me," she said, "there are about eight, I think. Oh, but I have forgotten M. Duval. That makes nine."

"So Duval is here?" His eyes were suddenly sharp. "Do you like the gentleman?"

She hesitated. "I am sorry if he is a friend of yours, sir, but I find him detestable."

"We think alike. And now tell me how long you have been here and if you have enjoyed your visit to Brighton?"

She told him they had been there three weeks, and then she changed the subject abruptly to inquiries after Lucinda and Frank instead of enlarging on the pleasures of the visit. She knew she should disapprove of a gentleman whose morals were open to question, but she found him a delightful companion and it was the first evening that she had enjoyed herself since she had come to Brighton. When he had finished his dinner he asked her if she played chess, and she said that she had not played for an age but would be happy to play with him if he did not object to a weak adversary.

"There is no adversary I like better after a day's travel," he assured her, and after the dishes were removed and the footman, by this time almost grovelling, returned to set out the chess table with its red and white pieces, they settled down to their game. They soon became so absorbed that they failed to notice the time until the carriages returned and Henrietta and her party walked into the room. She stopped short at seeing the two with their heads bent over the chess table.

"Lord Crayne!" she exclaimed. "I did not expect you until July."

"I thought I would surprise you, ma'am." He rose to his feet and waited for her to present him to her friends.

When this was done they all declared their weariness after a day at the races followed by a ball, and went off to bed, leaving Henrietta alone with the Miss Chevenings and the owner of the house. As the door closed behind the chattering French ladies she said with a slightly sharp note in her voice, "Your lordship should have warned me of your change in plans. I would have been here to welcome you."

"But nobody could have been more charming than this young lady," he assured her. "I am sorry that her brother is taking her and Miss Chevening home tomorrow."

It was on Maria's lips to retort that though Edward might take Liz he would not take her, when she recollected that they were now Lord Crayne's guests. She could only bow her acquiescence and take herself upstairs, and after thanking her host for the game of chess, Liz curtsied to him and his companion and followed her sister.

Henrietta asked his lordship when he had arrived.

"Earlier this evening."

"Mrs. Brenner knows you are here?"

"Yes. I told her I had engaged rooms at the castle for tonight."

"At the castle? But—why are you not there?"

"Frank and I traveled from Crayne to London and stayed a night in Manchester Square while Lucinda prepared for her journey to her aunt in Salisbury. She then accompanied us, breaking her journey here before going on with Frank to Salisbury tomorrow. Frank engaged rooms for the three of us at the castle—I wonder you did not see him there tonight?"

"If he was at the ball, there was a great crush and I scarcely saw anyone that I knew."

"Then how fortunate that you had your own party to

accompany you." He moved to the door. "I will leave you to your beauty sleep, my dear, and call on you in the morning."

Mme. St. Clair heard the door close behind him with a feeling of dismay. She had never seen him in so black a mood before, and she wondered if Liz had been tale-bearing in her absence. Then she consoled herself with the thought that she would be rid of everybody long before noon on the morrow—they would need no hints to speed their departure. And once the Chevenings had gone and she had him to herself, she would easily win him back to his customary good humor.

The ball in the castle assembly rooms having finished, Jasper made his way to the card room, where Rick Delamere was playing with some gentlemen from outside Brighton. All were fortifying themselves liberally with brandy against the long drive home. Jasper found his man bosky but able to understand when he asked if he intended to take Maria driving with him on the following morning.

"If the filly is willing to come," said Rick stupidly. "I'm always pleased to 'commodate a lady."

"But the lady tomorrow will not be my sister," said Jasper. "You might have another accident, Mr. Delamere, and I do not want to see another member of my family killed, as you killed my brother."

"What the devil do you mean?" Delamere got to his feet, swaying slightly and slopping his glass of brandy over the cards in front of him. "I had nothing to do with Vincent's death. Brought it on himself with his dam' bad driving."

"That is what you'd have people believe," said Jasper

clearly. "But you know quite well that you forced him through that fence to his death. Some might call it manslaughter, others by a stronger name, but I will simply demand your apology and that you will take back what you have just said."

"I'll do no such thing." Delamere threw the remains of his brandy in Jasper's face. "Take that for your insolence, Cornet Chevening, and keep out of my way in future if you do not want me to give you a thrashing."

"On the contrary," said Jasper coolly, taking out his handkerchief to wipe his face. "It is I who will administer the thrashing, Mr. Delamere, and I shall be happy to do it. You are too drunk to stand up tonight, but I suggest that you meet me tomorrow morning at eight on the race course, outside the grandstand, when you will have had time to sober up."

"What, are you challenging me to a bout with the gloves?" Delamere gave a roar of laughter and turned to invite the other gentlemen in the card room to join him, but a watchful silence reigned among them. All eyes were on the brash young man who was challenging the redoubtable Rick Delamere in such a reckless fashion. And even as they waited, Frank Crayne's voice broke the silence.

"So there you are, Jasper," he said pleasantly. "Your brother is looking for you. Did I hear you say something about a mill tomorrow morning on the race course? Will the sheriff allow it?"

"The sheriff will be in bed and snoring at that hour," said Jasper. "And you are right about the mill. I am meeting that—gentleman—there tomorrow at eight o'clock, and I would be obliged, Frank, if you will act as my second."

Frank tried to escape the dubious honor. "Should you not ask Edward?" he said. "He is staying here until tomorrow."

"No, he would stop the fight," murmured Jasper. "And I am not having that. I must have you." He raised his voice. "That is understood then, Delamere? You will meet me tomorrow?"

"Certainly, if you wish it." Rick had so far recovered himself to look Jasper up and down with studied contempt. "No doubt one of these gentlemen will be my second." As one of the gentlemen duly offered his services, Delamere continued, "I do not think Mr. Crayne need be nervous about the sheriff. He seldom visits Brighton and I do not anticipate the bout lasting long enough to attract any attention."

Jasper thanked Frank for his help and went back to the Ship Inn. "You can tell Edward what is going forward in the morning," he told Frank before he left. "But impress on him that nothing he can do or say will prevent me from meeting Delamere. My mind is set on it."

Frank did not wait until the morning before imparting the news of the encounter to his friend, and Edward took it with resignation.

"Jasper has been set on this for the past months," he remarked. "And it is better that he should meet Delamere and have done with it. I am only thankful it's to be fists on the race course and not pistols on the other side of the Channel. Jasper is no hand with a pistol."

"I am only concerned lest it is Jasper who will receive the thrashing," said Frank.

"The outcome is a matter of some concern either way," agreed Edward. "If Delamere wins it will be because Jasper is unable to stand on his feet by the end of it, but if it goes the other way Delamere will not forgive him, and he will take the first opportunity to even the score between them in a way that may not be particularly pleasant. He is devoid of scruples."

Frank agreed. "One cannot underrate him—he is not a clean fighter at the best of times. I am telling my man to spread word among the servants here of what is going forward, and I shall tell my uncle directly he returns from the Steine. We do not want to be confronted tomorrow morning by a crowd of roughs who will make short work of the three of us. Delamere would then hand out a few guineas apiece and finish with it, having taught Jasper a lesson in his own charming way."

"You think Lord Crayne will be there?"

"He will not miss it for the world. And there will be a crowd of onlookers, a referee, and a proper ring marked out—everything as it should be." Frank was taking his unwanted duties seriously and Edward appreciated it and hoped that Jasper did. As they mounted the stairs he asked when they had arrived in Brighton. "I did not see you at the ball," he said.

"We were too late for it and Lucinda wanted her bed."

"Is she with you then?"

"Yes. And you? What are your plans, beyond watching the mill tomorrow?"

"Oh," said Edward easily, "I am going to take my sisters home." He said goodnight and went to his room to find that the news of the impending fight had spread like wildfire through the hotel. "And the odds," added Tod lugubriously, "is all agin Mr. Jasper."

"Well, I daresay they are," agreed Edward, weary of his younger brother and his belligerency. Telling his servant to be sure and wake him in time he went to his bed, wishing he had been able to see Lucinda that evening and wondering if he would be able to talk to her in the morning.

The next day dawned with a clear sky and a soft breeze blowing over the downs, and at an early hour, when the air was sparkling fresh and the sea below glittering in the sunshine, the chain pier marching out into it like a necklace waiting for a woman's neck, a number of carts, carriages, horses and men could be seen making their way to the race course. Below them the countryside sloped down steeply to the town grouped along the Parade and the shore, the roofs of the houses of the quality blue-slated and staid, the flint cottages of the fisherfolk clustered behind.

While delighted to see the crowd already assembled, with the ring already strung with ropes and the square yard marked in the middle for the two antagonists, Frank experienced a few misgivings as he glanced at the other side and saw Delamere. He appeared more than ever tall, broad, and superbly confident, with his man Brodie beside him. It seemed to Frank that whichever way the fight went it was going to be unpleasant for Jasper, and he secretly hoped that neither would win, that, in short, it might end with them shaking hands—each man aware of having met his equal in strength and skill.

He had got thus far in his thoughts when a hand was laid on his shoulder and he turned to find his uncle beside him.

"Thank 'ee, Frank my boy," said his lordship with a chuckle. "Good of you to send that message to my rooms last night. Is that your man?"

"Jasper Chevening, sir."

"I'd like to meet your pugilistic friend." The introduction was made and Lord Crayne said he had had the pleasure of playing chess with Jasper's sister the evening before. "Your youngest sister, I believe, sir. A charmin' young lady, 'pon my soul."

With the lack of enthusiasm characteristic of the Chevening males—save Edward—when their female relatives were praised, Jasper agreed casually that Liz was developing into quite a passable young woman. Edward joined them then and was greeted warmly. The referee asked if the two gentlemen were ready. Delamere peeled off his coat and Jasper did likewise.

"They're betting heavily on Rick," Edward told his brother as he took his coat from him. "Surprise 'em, Jasper."

"I intend to," said Jasper, and ignored the derisive cheer that greeted him as he stepped into the ring.

Delamere, though broader and taller than Jasper, was not in as good condition. Jasper's training had stood him in good stead, and the fight that should have lasted ten rounds at least was sorely disappointing to the onlookers. The first round was sufficient to change the betting from Delamere to Chevening, the second had Rick fighting viciously, and the third had him on his knees. Brodie whispered fiercely as he helped him up, "Get him in the groin, Mr. Delamere, sir. It ain't a prize fight so there's no rules."

Rick Delamere took his servant's advice and sent Jasper down doubled up; but there appeared to be certain rules that had to be observed after all. The referee stepped forward, declared it to be a foul, and warned the larger protagonist that another breach of the rules would give the victory to Cornet Chevening.

Jasper got back on his feet and let his fury add to the science recently acquired from ex-champion Tod, with the result that by the end of the fourth round it did not seem likely that Mr. Delamere would be showing his face in Brighton or anywhere else for some weeks to come.

"Now," Jasper said as he stood over his adversary, who was sitting on the grass spitting blood into his handkerchief and ignoring the shouts from the crowd to get up like a man, "perhaps you will refrain from spreading lies about my dead brother."

"Damned if I do." Speaking indistinctly, Delamere was still able to return Jasper's glance with a look of hate. "I'll kill you for this, Jasper Chevening."

"If you succeed," said Jasper with a ferocious grin, "I shall be sorry that I'm not there to see you hang." And then Frank bustled him off to his uncle's carriage where Edward was waiting with its owner and Tod.

Fifteen

Maria, determined to sulk until the carriage was there to take them to Chevening, remained in her room for breakfast, and as Henrietta never came downstairs for what she called an uncivilized meal, Liz entered the breakfast room that morning to find it empty. The servant who brought her coffee and hot rolls told her that the rest of Madam's guests had left.

"What, all of them?" The astonishment in her voice provoked an awkward grin from the man as he replied that everyone had gone at an early hour.

He had only just left the room when Lucinda walked in, and a glance at her friend's face told Liz that she was in a very bad temper.

"Where is Frank?" she demanded, scarcely acknowledging Liz's greeting, and then, "No, don't tell me. He is still up there on the race course watching that mill!"

"A mill?" Liz found it hard to understand why Frank

184

Crayne should be watching a windmill at that time of the morning.

"A fight, child!" said Lucinda impatiently. "Directly Merrydew told me there was to be a mill up there this morning I knew we should not start out for Salisbury for hours. *Men!*" She flung off her lace mantle and plaited straw hat and sat herself down. Liz offered her breakfast, which she accepted. "I was too angry to eat a mouthful before I came out," she confessed with a slightly softened air.

"Brothers are sometimes not very considerate," said Liz, thinking of Vincent. "Though I must except my dear Edward."

Lucinda appeared to think nothing of Edward. "Of course my uncle was there too," she went on. "His man pretended he did not know where he was. 'Nonsense,' I said. 'He's up on the race course with Mr. Frank and you know it as well as I do.' That coffee smells good."

Liz poured some out for her and watched her while she set about hot rolls and honey with an appetite.

"I am starving," she said frankly. "I never eat before a journey and as we were to start at half-past eight I thought we would breakfast on the way. But no man ever thinks of a female if there is a chance of seeing a prize fight. If His Majesty were not in London no doubt he would have been there too." The coffee seemed to be taking some of the fire out of her. "How long are you staying?" she asked.

Liz told her that Edward was to take them home that day. "The carriage is to come for us at noon."

"Do not build your hopes on that. I have known these fights to last five or six hours."

"Oh dear, but we must leave today," Liz said, dismayed. "Especially now that Lord Crayne is in Brighton."

"I do not suppose Uncle Herbert would object to entertaining two pretty girls for an extra few days," said Lucinda briefly. "But Mme. St. Clair might not be so pleased." She added with some curiosity, "I conclude that you did not know before you came here that this house belonged to my uncle?"

Liz shook her head vigorously. "We were told a friend had lent it to Cousin Henrietta for the summer. Had she known the true situation Mamma would not have dreamed of allowing us to come." Her eyes were round with horror at the thought of what Lady Chevening would have had to say about it. "Directly I discovered it I wrote to Edward begging him to come and take us home, and he arrived yesterday." She added with some diffidence, "None of us knew that your uncle and Mamma's cousin were—old friends."

Lucinda drank her coffee thoughtfully. "My uncle married when he was very young," she said between sips. "My aunt was said to be very beautiful and charming, and he was desperately in love with her. She died after they had been married a year, with the birth of a son who did not survive. My uncle never married again, and her rooms at Crayne are still as she left them. A few years ago he met Mme. St. Clair in Paris and found her gay, attractive, and amusing, and he became her lover. As he found happiness in her company, neither Frank nor I could censure him. In his fashion, he remains constant to his dead wife, and I am very much attached to him. Madame has her uses, although he has to pay dearly for her favors. I expect she is here for money; she usually is."

Liz said that she thought she had come for Ann-Marie's dowry, and Lucinda gave a small laugh.

"Her demands are increasing," she said. "I trust she will not persuade him to part with the money he has promised for *my* dowry."

"It would not be very fair if he did!"

Lucinda shrugged her shoulders. "My dear child, gentlemen are seldom fair in their dealings with females. As a whole, I detest them. I have not found one yet I like better than Frank, and at times *he* aggravates me so much that I could sieze him by the hair and bang his head against the nearest wall!"

The sound of approaching wheels sent her running to the window. "They are back!" she cried, and a few minutes later Lord Crayne, followed by Frank, Edward and Jasper, entered the house. The girls heard Frank's voice demanding beef steak from Mrs. Brenner, and then the breakfast-room door opened and the gentlemen entered.

Miss Crayne scarcely troubled herself to drop them a curtsy before speaking her mind. "So you have all been up on the race course this morning, gentlemen, to enjoy the elevating spectacle of two of your kind fighting each other. I must congratulate you on your taste. It appears to have wholly escaped Frank's memory that he was to start for Salisbury with me at half-past eight this morning."

"My dear," said Lord Crayne pacifically, "Frank had pledged himself to support a friend, and I am glad that he did. I have seldom seen better fighting between amateurs. They were pretty evenly matched, but the cornet here had a quickness of action that the other had forgotten, if he ever knew it. Cornet Chevening's punches were remarkable. I was delighted to be a spectator at such an encounter."

Liz, who had been staring at her brother, now broke in with a dismayed exclamation that his right eye was cut and bleeding.

"It formed a close acquaintance with a gentleman's fist," said Jasper, laughing a little ruefully. But Lucinda showed him that she thought it no laughing matter. She whirled round on Edward, saying, "I conclude, Mr. Chevening, that your brother—"

"Was one of the two concerned? I must admit that he was, ma'am," said Edward with an amusement that added to her wrath.

"And who was the other?" she demanded.

"You will learn that in due course, my dear," said her uncle smoothly. "May I suggest that you take Miss Elizabeth Chevening into the drawing room upstairs while your brother has his breakfast? As for your journey to Salisbury, there is a new carriage in my coach-house here that you will find more comfortable than the one in which we traveled from Crayne."

Lucinda was not to be so easily appeased. She flounced out of the room with Liz, stopping short at sight of Frank, followed by the footman, who was bearing a piece of raw steak on a plate. "That," she said, "is for Jasper's eye, I conclude?"

"Why yes." Frank chuckled. "It was the only place he was marked. You should see the fellow he was fighting. His face looks like a map of London."

"Thank you, I do not wish to hear any more about it." As Lucinda went up the stairs to the front drawing room with Liz, the latter whispered that she thought Jasper must have been fighting a brother officer. "For they would not dare have a bout near London," she told Miss Crayne. "His colonel is very strict about such matters."

Lucinda spent the next half-hour or so walking up and down the drawing room, impatiently ready to start off for Salisbury directly Frank had swallowed his breakfast. She was not pleased to hear the continual bursts of laughter coming from the breakfast room beneath, and went to the window overlooking the Steine.

When the door behind her opened she did not turn her head. "So you have finally finished?" she said. "I hope you did not hurry your breakfast, and now perhaps we can start for Salisbury two hours later than I had planned."

"I have come to make Jasper's apologies for having detained Frank so long," said Edward Chevening in his quiet way. "I hope you will forgive him."

She faced him angrily. "I asked you not very long ago if you could not control your younger brother," she said.

"And I told you that I had tried," he replied mildly. "But even I find him uncontrollable at times."

She did not smile. "Was it Delamere?" she asked, and then, as he did not answer, "So it was! Jasper was very foolish and Rick Delamere will not forget this morning's work. I have seldom seen a gentleman more cock-a-hoop than your brother was this morning, and though I dislike his antagonist I find no pleasure in hearing that his face has been smashed. With my knowledge of your family, I suppose it should not have surprised me."

Her words cut him sharply. He said coldly, "I regret that my relatives do not please you."

"How can anyone be pleased with a family whose members are so heartless?" she demanded. "But it is not only this morning that has influenced me. In St. James's Square last summer I was standing near Maria at her coming-out ball when somebody congratulated her on its brilliance, and your sister laughed and said it was not for her but 'for our little moneybag yonder,' nodding to Sarah Wakefield."

"And you judged my entire family by the excited and thoughtless remark of a girl of seventeen?" Perceiving that he was extremely angry in his turn, she checked for a moment. She had never seen him so aroused before.

"Lucinda," he went on sternly, "you are determined to quarrel with me whenever we meet. Are you still angry with me for what I tried to say to you that last day of your stay at Edgecombe two years ago? I knew when I mended your earring for you that I was in danger of falling in love with you—I, a second son, and you with your uncle's high hopes for a brilliant marriage. But that morning I had received a letter from my father demanding my immediate return to London, and I was apprehensive that it had to do with Vincent. I was afraid that he would do what he had threatened to do before—send Vincent abroad and myself with him. I knew if that happened I might be away for some time—that I would not be able to see you at all during your first London Season. Because I cared so much I tried to warn you—clumsily, I admit—of the treacherous world into which you were going, a world that I detest. I am afraid I did not succeed very well, for when I returned I found you changed indeed. Yet, beneath the affected manners and insincerity that you obviously learned, I could catch glimpses of the Lucinda who had meant so much to me. Is it too late to hope that she will forget her 'fashionable' ways . . . that she does really know in her heart how worthless they are?"

He paused, and she waited a moment before she could control herself enough to speak. Then she said in a low voice, "And you, a Chevening, dare to preach to me! After the way you all behaved to Sarah after Vincent's death. Nobody troubled themselves to discover if she was suffering, if she was heartbroken. She was bundled off like a piece of goods that had lost its value to Lady Stroud——"

"Who received her with love and warm generosity," he reminded her.

"But Sarah was shut out of your family circle all the same. Do you wonder that she concluded she had only been embraced because of the fortune she would inherit? Can you doubt that when she was offered a home at Edgecombe, your parents were already considering the size of that fortune, which they had determined would be shared with one of their sons? Vincent's wicked and cruel letter confirmed this in her mind, and it is no wonder that she hates you all and asked her grandfather to give her a home as far away from Kent as possible. You have accused me of insincerity, Mr. Chevening, but I accuse you and your family of hypocrisy. When they gave that child of eight years a home at Edgecombe, it was as if they were welcoming the assured provider of future wealth. The Chevenings have no souls."

"You have a high opinion of us indeed." Shocked pride gave a new austerity to his voice. "You have said enough. I will only wish you goodbye and a pleasant journey to Salisbury." At the door he turned and said, with a grim smile, "And I give you joy of the Salisbury curates."

When Frank came to find his sister to tell her that he was ready to start, he found her with tears on her cheeks.

"Now what have you been at?" he asked. "I saw Edward come down the stairs a short while ago with a face like thunder. I hope you have not been quarreling with him again, for he is one of the finest fellows I know."

After his nephew and niece had gone, Lord Crayne climbed the stairs to Henrietta's dressing room and found her very much annoyed.

"Your niece has taken the new carriage with my favorite lining," she complained.

"I have lent it to her for her journey to Salisbury," said Herbert Crayne, seating himself in a chair from where he could watch her as she selected earrings and a necklace with scrupulous care. He wondered how often Duval had sat there doing the same thing. "When you wrote from Paris mentioning the two young ladies you wished to entertain here, you spoke of some small business matter you wished to discuss with me when we met?"

"Oh yes." She smiled at him before returning to her jewel case and then to the study of her reflection in the mirror, with first this necklace and then that held up against her throat. "It is about Ann-Marie's dowry. You know I told you of the excellent match I have made for her?"

"With one of the new French aristocracy. Yes, you told me." He waited for her to continue.

"Naturally the family want a dowry with Ann-Marie," went on Mme. St. Clair lightly. "And as my poor husband has no money I have come to you, the dearest friend a woman ever had." It was evident that she thought the fight he had witnessed that morning with so much enjoyment had banished his ill humor of the night before. She dismissed all men as being schoolboys at heart.

"Forgive me if I am wrong," he said with urbanity, "but Ann-Marie is your husband's daughter, is she not? She is certainly not mine, and under the circumstances surely her dowry is M. St. Clair's business?"

"Now Herbert, dearest, do not be difficult." Henrietta

frowned. "You know that St. Clair has no money and the dowry is to be five thousand pounds. It has all been settled. If he were to find such a sum he would be forced to sell his estate."

"Then I suggest that he sell it. If you have put your hand to the contract there is nothing else he can do."

"When you are in this mood, my dearest Herbert," said Henrietta, settling at last for a necklace and earrings of turquoise in gold settings, "I pay no attention to you."

"But I am afraid on this occasion you will have to pay attention to me. I have at last freed myself from the burden of my father's extravagance and I am not prepared to put my neck into another noose. You are greedy, Henrietta, and it has amused me from time to time to indulge you, but I am not paying your husband's debts. There is another alternative, of course." Then, as she looked at him expectantly, "St. Clair could sell the Paris house and you could live in the château with him instead." He examined his nails with care. "How long are you proposing to stay in Brighton after the Miss Chevenings leave today?"

She stared at him, flushing with surprise. "I will leave tomorrow if you wish it," she said, and then as he remained unsmiling she went on with sudden misgiving, "Have you found another lady whose company is preferable to mine?"

There had always been another lady—an eighteen-year-old wife lying in the family vault at Crayne. He had managed to dull that image from time to time when he was with Mme. St. Clair, beautiful to look at, amusing to be with and selfish and vain at heart, with greedy hands held out always asking for jewels and clothes and carriages. He did not know why, but he was suddenly thoroughly weary of her and her demands. It might have been the game of chess with Liz Chevening that had brought his wife back so vividly to his mind. The child had been dressed in a lavender-colored muslin gown with lace ruffles at the throat and wrists, and emanated a simplicity that his young wife had favored all those years ago contrasting sharply with Henrietta's smart and vulgar house-party, the abominable Duval strutting there as if he owned the house.

"Will you be leaving from Dover?" he asked, getting up. "Or from Folkestone? I hear that the passage from Brighton to the French coast can be delightful at this time of year. Order a carriage when you wish, my dear. I am returning to Crayne. I am selling this house immediately; Frank and Lucinda have never liked it."

Sixteen

It was a subdued party that started out for Chevening Place that morning. Jasper had left for London earlier, and Edward was glad that he had brought his carriage as he took the reins from Tod to drive it out of Brighton. The Parade was thronged in the forenoon of the lovely summer's day; all the ladies of fashion were out for an airing beside a sea that rippled in lazily to wash the pebbles on the shore.

As Edward drove with Tod beside him, he guessed that word would soon be passed from the Parade to the Steine that Sir William Chevening's heir had come to fetch his sisters home. And none too soon, no doubt the gossips would say, discussing the notorious Mme. St. Clair's house party and M. Duval in particular, a profligate, if ever there was one.

The explanation that Edward gave at Chevening for

their sudden arrival that evening was that more guests had
arrived and his sisters' good manners demanded that they
should give way to them. Fortunately they did not deny
it, although Maria openly sulked and went off to bed
early, saying that the journey in Edward's small carriage
had given her a headache.

The following morning Edward went to see Lady Stroud
and had a long talk with her about Sarah before taking
his carriage back to Sloane Street. The girls resettled themselves at Chevening, Liz receiving a rapturous welcome
from her little dog Posy and openly rejoicing to be home,
and Maria still sulking and refusing to say why.

On reading the *Courier* a few days later, Sir William
noted an item in the society column that aroused his interest. It described a most unusual duel on the Brighton
race course between two young gentlemen, who, instead
of crossing the Channel to indulge in the use of pistols,
had surprisingly used their fists. One young gentleman,
a certain cornet with the initials J. C., had given the other
gentleman, Mr. R. D., a severe trouncing, to the surprise of
the latter's friends, with whom the gentleman had a reputation for being no mean performer with the gloves. Mr.
R. D. was now recovering, with his face severely marked
and a body equally severely bruised, while his antagonist
escaped with scarcely a scratch.

"So that was it!" said Sir William with a wry grin. "No
wonder Edward removed his sisters. Did he think I was
fool enough to believe his botched-up excuses? But what
the devil was Jasper up to?"

Maria had been too uncommunicative since she returned
home to help him, and he did not wish Sophia to see the
offending paragraph, so he tucked the newspaper under
his arm and went to find Liz. She was on the lower

terrace happily throwing sticks for Posy to fetch. The small dog had become much too fat in her absence, the footman who had been told to take her for walks having skimped his duty.

"So, Liz," Sir William said in mock anger, "you did not come home because Mme. St. Clair's house was over-full after all?"

She looked confused. "I am sorry, Papa, but I don't think Edward wanted Mamma to know the truth about Lord Crayne."

"Crayne! What in heavens' name had he to do with it?"

"It was his house in which we were staying."

"Lord Crayne's house?" He took her arm. "Supposing we sit on this seat for a few minutes and let Posy rest while you tell me about it." They sat there comfortably while Posy flung herself down beside them, her plump sides going like a small bellows.

"After we had been there for nearly three weeks," said Liz, "I discovered that the house was his. Maria said she had known for some time, but I wrote to Edward to ask him to take us away because I guessed Mme. St. Clair to be Lord Crayne's mistress." She glanced at her father to see if he were shocked, but as he remained unmoved she went on with more courage. "I think she asked us there as a—" She hesitated and he suggested quietly: "A cloak, perhaps, to cover certain other activities?"

"Yes, Papa, that is what I meant. I would have written to Mamma, but I was afraid that if she discovered how she had been deceived she would come over herself, and she would have had a great deal to say to Cousin Henrietta before we left."

Sir William could see the force of this argument. "And now perhaps you can enlighten me on another question," he said. "Why did Jasper think it necessary to fight Mr. Delamere on the morning you left?"

"I did not know that it was Delamere!" Liz was shocked. "Oh, dear, please do not tell Maria. She probably thinks as I did that Jasper fought one of his brother officers and they chose the Brighton race course because it was far away from London."

It was too late to prevent Maria from discovering it, however. She had visited her Aunt Stroud, who showed her the paragraph in the *Courier*. Maria had ridden home in a rage, arriving with her horse in a lather, her whip nearly broken, and her temper boiling over. Seeing her father and Liz walking into the house together, she dismounted, threw the reins of her ill-used mount to her groom, and came to meet them.

"Have you seen the *Courier* this morning?" she demanded. "That paragraph about Jasper fighting Rick? But I can see from your faces that you have. No wonder Rick has not written to you, Papa! How could Jasper have done such a wicked thing?" And she burst into tears.

"Come, my dear!" Her father put his arm round her. "This will not do. I am trying to discover why Jasper fought Mr. Delamere, and it seems you may be able to throw some light on it."

"Indeed I can!" Angrily she drew away from him. "On the night of the castle ball Rick told me that his tiresome wife was dead at last, and he asked me to marry him and I accepted him. He was going to write for your consent the next day and I could not think why you had not received his letter. Now I understand. Jasper must have got wind of our engagement and used it as an excuse to pick a quarrel with Rick."

"I do not believe it." Sir William was more perplexed still. "I cannot see my youngest son, fool as he is, taking it upon himself to knock the heads off young men who propose for his sisters. There must be more to it than that."

Maria looked at him tentatively. "Then . . . you will give your consent to my marriage with Rick?"

"I suppose I shall." He did not sound overjoyed at the prospect. "I would not stand in the way of the happiness of any of my children, but I cannot say I would have chosen Delamere for you. I am afraid your mother is not going to find it easy to love him."

"She is not required to love him," said Maria with a laugh. "If I love him, that is all that matters." And she went indoors to change from her riding dress.

Sir William left Liz to throw more sticks for Posy and went to write a lengthy letter to Edward, in which he asked if there were any explanation for his brother's meeting with Delamere other than Maria's engagement to the man. Edward did not reply for some days, and Sir William waited in growing irritation for his reply. When at last it came it was short and singularly unhelpful, shedding no light at all on the matter.

"My dear Father," Edward wrote. *"It must have been highly vexatious for you to read the account of Jasper's meeting with Delamere in a newspaper. I can assure you that it had nothing to do with Maria and I am afraid that his reason for challenging Delamere is of a private nature that I am unable to divulge. I trust my mother and sisters are well and that you too are in good health. Your dutiful son, Edward Chevening."*

Sir William did not feel himself to be in good health at all as he finished reading his son's letter; in fact, he felt as if a fit of apoplexy might strike him down at any moment.

During the days that followed his encounter with Delamere, Jasper became irritated by the number of times that Frank Crayne called at his lodgings with the excuse of asking how his eye did, or simply saying that he happened to be in the neighborhood. Edward was mysteriously out of town for a week, and when he returned Jasper complained to him about his friend's behavior.

"Frank seems to think I need a watchdog," he said. "Directly you had left—without telling anyone where you went, by the way—he arrived back from Salisbury and has been haunting me like a ghost. I cannot stir without him. I would be obliged if you will tell him that I am well able to take care of myself."

"You are an ungrateful young dog, are you not?" said Edward.

"I daresay I am, but anyone would think from the way he behaves that I should not step outside my lodgings without a bodyguard." Jasper was still indignant. "I know what is in his mind and in yours. You both think that Delamere will set his ruffians on to me."

"That is what we both fear," said Edward.

"And what do you suggest I should do? Should I perhaps travel like visiting royalty, with an armed escort?"

"When you come to see me here at Sloane Street at night I would advise you to ride, and have your servant ride close to you," Edward told him seriously. "There is only one watch house in this district and the constables there are usually drunk. I really should mind what I was about, my dear fellow."

Jasper departed in a dudgeon and Edward was left to cogitate on the ingratitude of man. He went up to his gallery to find comfort in his collection, but somehow even the Raphael had lost its charm today. His eyes went to the small bronze horse and he took it from its shelf, remembering how Lucinda had said it was like her little horse at Crayne. He had ceased being angry with her for her impassioned defense of Sarah Wakefield, and he could not put her from his mind. It seemed to him sometimes Vincent's long shadow was to be cast over his life as long as he lived.

Frank having been summoned to Crayne Castle, Edward paid a visit to Chevening to make his peace with his father, who greeted him shortly and spent most of his time in the justice room, thus showing his displeasure. His mother as usual had a slightly abstracted welcome for him, and Maria would not speak to him.

Only Liz was happy to see him, and as she walked with him one morning to see Lady Stroud, she told him that Maria had been writing constantly to Delamere since their return and had received no reply to her letters. "It looks to me as if he wishes to have no more to do with her," Liz said. Edward said that in that case he was sorry for Maria if she really loved him, but thankful as far as the family was concerned.

Sir William, meanwhile, was slightly conscience-stricken over the way he had snubbed his son's overtures at peacemaking. If Jasper had quarreled with Delamere, he thought, it was his business and not his brother's. He wrote to Jasper, telling him to meet him in Dover Street on the following Friday. When he arrived, looking as handsome as ever, Sir William came to the point without delay.

"If you have no ambitions beyond your cornetcy," he

said severely, "perhaps you will tell me why you fought Delamere on Brighton race course the morning that Edward brought his sisters home? Edward is as close as an oyster about it, and when my sons make spectacles of themselves for the entertainment of others, I like to know the reason for it."

Jasper flushed, hesitated, and then told him of the suspicions he had that Delamere had planned the upset that killed Vincent. When he had done, he saw that his father was looking extremely angry.

"Do you imagine that *I* did not examine Hookey over the whole business?" the baronet asked. "Hookey was a good groom; his one passion in life was horses. He loved those bays of Vincent's—they were his world—and if there had been anything untoward about the accident he would have told me. I do not believe for one moment that Delamere intended to force Vincent through that fence. Vincent happened to hit the fence, which was rotten, and down he went. According to Hookey, Vincent's driving was every bit as bad as Delamere's."

"And you believe him, sir?" Jasper was crestfallen.

"I do." Sir William was now very much the Roman parent. "And I am extremely angry that you should have the temerity to make an enemy of Rick Delamere over the whole affair. You will oblige me by keeping out of his way, and if there are any family quarrels to be taken up in future you will approach me first."

Jasper was dismissed, considerably chastened.

That same morning Edward's cook was out early buying fish and vegetables in the local market. She was annoyed because Tod had not allowed the young groom to accompany her to carry her basket, and she accepted the aid of a stranger with a gush of thanks. She was a stout lady and short of breath.

"It's that Tod," she told her rescuer. "The man-servant in the 'ouse in Sloane Street where I'm cook. Sometimes 'is 'ighness will let the groom come with me to carry me basket, and sometimes 'e won't. This morning, 'Ho,' 'e says, 'h'I'm sorry, Mrs. Paddock,' 'e says, 'but h'I've other things for Bob 'ere to do. Take one of them maids with you,' 'e says. Telling me what to do—it was like 'is impertence. 'Thank you, Mr. Tod,' I says dignified-like. 'I'll go alone.'"

"How fortunate then, Mrs. Paddock, as I'm going in the d'rection of Sloane Street myself," said the stranger. "I can carry that basket all the way. It's far too 'eavy for a lady like you, and I wonders at your Mr. Tod for allowing of it." Affable and polite, he took the heavy basket from her, and as they walked they talked about their employers. Later she thought they had talked more about hers than his, but she was sure he was employed by a gentleman, he was so polite.

Mr. Chevening, she told him, was a quiet gentleman, not given to much entertaining, which was a good thing, though he had a brother what was an officer at the barracks what seemed to look on the house as if it was his own.

"Walks in and out at all times," she said. "''Ave you got anything for dinner today, Mrs. Paddock?,' 'e says. 'If it's mutton, mind it ain't tough and don't spill your gin over it.' Impertent young gentleman, is Mr. Jasper, but you can't help laughing at 'im all the same. 'You git out of my kitchen, Mr. Jasper,' I says, 'afore I takes my rolling pin to you,' and off he goes laughing 'is 'ead off."

The stranger sympathized. "Young gentlemen is all the

same," he told her. "I s'pose 'e stays out late as they all do? Playing cards most like till daybreak?"

"Not with Mr. Edward Chevening," said Mrs. Paddock, " 'E ain't for cards. 'E's wrapped up in what 'e calls 'is collection—a lot of old bits of chiny and statues and picshurs—you never see sich things in your life."

"A lot of gentlemen set store on picshurs, Mrs. Paddock," said her companion smoothly. "So Mr. Jasper goes off early from Sloane Street, does 'e?"

" 'E generally leaves at midnight," agreed Mrs. Paddock. " 'E's coming to dinner tonight, which is why I bought fish for 'im. As a rule Mr. Edward Chevening don't care for fish."

"I dessay Mr. Jasper 'as a kerridge," said the stranger. "These young gentlemen don't walk a yard if they can 'elp it."

"Bless you, Mr. Jasper ain't got no kerridge. 'E's only at the barracks, Mr.—" She waited for him to give his name, but he did not oblige her, and she went on, "Sometimes 'e comes on foot but more often 'is servant comes with him on 'orseback."

They had reached her destination, and the stranger carried the heavy basket down the area steps. "I shall look for you in the market tomorrer, ma'am," said Mr. Brodie, and with a somewhat wolfish smile he took himself off.

It could not have been half an hour before dinner was ready to be put on the table that Jasper sent word he was detained and could not be with his brother that night. "A petticoat," thought Edward, hoping it was not Mrs. Porter, but his annoyance was dispersed by the sight of Frank, who had came by on his way from visiting an old friend of the Winters in Richmond.

"I called in," he told his friend, "to assure myself that all was well with Jasper."

Edward told him that Jasper was fighting-fit. "And now that you are here," he added, "you may as well eat his dinner as he has just sent word that he will not be coming tonight."

Frank was delighted to do so, and during the meal he told him the latest news of his family. Lucinda was still in Salisbury. "She sent a message for you in her last letter," he added. "I was to tell you that she had heard from Sarah Wakefield, who wrote that your Yorkshire visit had made her very happy. I was also to tell you that our aunt in Salisbury says that Lucinda is creating a disturbance among the curates there, but she has not discovered one yet that she would like to marry. She is, however, attracted by the archdeacon, who I gather is a handsome man, preaches very popular sermons, and is unmarried."

Edward felt he could afford to laugh at the archdeacon in the face of the rest of Lucinda's message.

"So that is where you went that week," Frank said curiously. "To Yorkshire."

"Yes," said Edward. "From something Lucinda said I thought I would go to my Aunt Stroud for information concerning Sarah, and what she had to tell me sent me to Yorkshire. I was very unsure of my reception but determined to straighten out any tangle between her family and mine. I found her ready to listen and ready to forgive, and she presented me to her aunt and to her grandfather, a fine old fellow who made me extremely welcome. I left them feeling that Sarah could not be happier or in better hands. It was a great weight off my mind, because we had all been very neglectful of her."

Frank nodded his approval. "Lucinda can be apt sometimes," he said with feeling.

It was just on midnight when Frank went down the steps to mount his waiting horse. After shouting a farewell to Edward at the window above, he moved off with his groom into the shadows between the lighted entranceway and the nearest street lamp.

Less than ten minutes later, his groom was back alone, banging desperately on the door.

Seventeen

Early the following morning, an urgent message from Edward had Sir William out of bed, dressed, and in his carriage in the space of fifteen minutes. He arrived in Sloane Street as speedily as the horses could take him.

Edward was watching for him and opened the door himself. He was unshaven and still in his clothes of the night before. The front of his shirt and his cravat were stained with blood.

"Edward, my dear fellow, what on earth has happened?" asked his father.

"Frank Crayne was attacked after he left my house last night." Edward took him into the breakfast room where a scared little maid was only just unbolting the shutters. "Four or five ruffians set on him and his servant, dragged Frank from his horse, kicked and beat him and left him half-dead, and then ran off. Fortunately the ringleader went straight into the arms of the watch and they have him under lock and key. The groom came off lightly because the brutes only seemed intent on preventing him from coming to his master's rescue. But Frank is badly injured. I sent Tod to Sir Berkeley, telling him what had happened, and he came in all haste, but the physician he brought with him is an old woman—his only thought appeared to be to bleed poor Frank, who had lost enough blood already."

"Frank is here then?"

"Oh yes. He cannot be moved. Tod and I made a rough litter and carried him back here and up to my bedroom, while my young groom helped his man with the horses, who were likely to bolt."

"What did Sir Berkeley's man say?"

"You know what these London physicians are like. He shook his head and doubted if he would last until morning. He was convinced he had cracked his skull. After he had gone I sent Tod for a surgeon I know in Clapham, begging him to come as soon as he could. He is with him now." Edward stared unseeingly at the neat little garden beyond the breakfast room window. "That this should have happened to Frank of all people."

"He is the last of his line, is he not?"

"He is the only male descendant. There have been Craynes at Crayne Castle since the Conquest."

"Have you written to Lord Crayne?"

"Sir Berkeley is doing that, and he is starting off for Salisbury today to break the news to Lucinda and to bring her back with him. I don't know how I can face them. It was Jasper's folly in antagonizing Delamere that has led to this."

"You mean Delamere had a hand in the attack on Frank? Surely not!"

"The man the watch caught last night was Delamere's man, Brodie," said Edward briefly.

Sir William was too shocked to speak, and at that moment Dr. Gordon came downstairs and they went into the hall to him.

"How bad is he?" asked Edward anxiously.

"Bad enough, sir." The surgeon tried to speak cheerfully. "To enumerate what is wrong—he has a broken leg and five broken ribs, but I do not think the skull is cracked. There is a deep gash that time and careful nursing should heal. The ruffians must have hit him wherever they could reach him."

"Do you think he should be bled any more?"

"When the ribs are broken bleeding is essential, as near the broken bones as possible. Your London gentleman is right there."

"But will he live?"

Dr. Gordon hesitated. "In all such cases there is a risk of fever, and he will need a nurse with him day and night. He looks to be a young man who has not indulged in excesses, however, and his physical strength may bring him through. In the meantime, if you will direct me to the nearest leather merchant I will have two splints made for his leg. Lengths of leather are all that are necessary, lightly tied with a twelve-tail bandage or two to keep the limb still. I have put an adhesive plaster on the ribs, but when he recovers consciousness he will be in great pain. I have left an opiate with your man Tod with directions how it is to be administered. He appears to be a sensible fellow."

Sir William took Dr. Gordon to the leather merchant himself, and after the splint had been fitted and tied in place the surgeon departed, saying that he would call the

next day. Sir William advised Edward to eat some breakfast, and went off to Dover Street to have his own. After-
wards, he called again at Sloane Street to ask if there was
anything he could have sent from Chevening for the
injured man.

"Ask Mamma if she knows of anyone in the village
with a knowledge of the sickroom who would be willing
to come and help me to nurse Frank." There was a desperate note in Edward's voice. "The hospital nurse that
Sir Berkeley's physician sent us was a dreadful old hag,
extremely dirty, and the first thing she said was that if
she was expected to sit up nights she would need plenty
of brandy to keep her going. I told her she need not
trouble to unpack her bag."

"I will ask your mamma," said Sir William. "If she
does not know of someone perhaps Minnie will—she has
lived longer in Chevening and knows the village better.
But in the meantime, what will you do?"

"In the daytime Tod and I will take turns in sitting
with Frank," Edward said. "And I shall have a mattress
on the floor beside his bed at night. There is not much we
can do beyond keeping him comfortable and as free from
pain as possible."

Sir William put the problem to his wife when he arrived home, and her answer was direct and unequivocal.
"I know of nobody," she said, "and I shall look for nobody. I want no old crone who will be sick on the journey
and require as much waiting on in the finish as poor
Frank himself."

"Then perhaps Minnie," hazarded Sir William, and was
again taken up sharply.

"Minnie is having no part in this," said Sophia. "Maria!
Stop mooning over that stupid novel and sit down and

write to your Aunt Stroud. Tell her that Mr. Crayne was attacked in the street last night and is now lying dangerously ill in your brother's house. Ask her to come here and take my place while I go to Eddy."

As she left the room the girls stared at each other in astonishment. "It is the first time anyone has called Edward Eddy since our grandmother died," said Liz in an awed voice, while Maria tried to gather her wits sufficiently to write her letter.

Lady Chevening in the meantime went into action like a frigate with all guns at the ready. Corrie, who had been the family's nurse and became head sewing maid when Liz entered the schoolroom, was summoned and told to pack linen sheets, towels, and a bag for her own needs. The housekeeper was given a list of the things her ladyship wished to take with her; the butler was bustled off to find the best wines and brandy; the poultry-keeper had a message delivered to him for baskets of eggs and young cockerels to be killed and ready for an early start in the morning.

When Sophia arrived in Sloane Street, Tod, who was teaching the cook how to prepare a bowl of broth, called to one of the maids to run and tell her master that two of the Chevening carriages were outside.

The girl ran up with the message and Edward came at once, thinking that his mother had sent somebody to help with the nursing. He arrived in the hall as the servant opened the front door, and to his amazement, found his mother on the doorstep.

Behind her was the redoubtable Corrie, and then came Chevening servants bearing baskets of eggs, fresh butter and plump chicken, while behind them a footman carried a huge basket containing cordials, bottles of wine, brandy and black currant jelly and anything else from the butler's cellars and the housekeeper's storerooms that could be recommended for an invalid.

"Well, Eddy my dear," Sophia said, smiling at him as he stood there too surprised to speak. "I have brought Corrie, who will take turns with me in nursing Frank, and some things from Chevening that we shall find useful."

"Mamma!" He caught her hands and they were withdrawn gently, in order to caress his face.

"I have come myself," she said. "And together we shall hope to get him better. You may take me to Frank at once, while Corrie sees to the storing away of the things we have brought with us. Is he conscious?"

"He has been conscious on and off since late last night, but he is in great pain and the surgeon says there is now some fever."

"There usually is, I believe, with broken bones," Sophia said comfortingly. "I will see him, but now that I am here I am in charge and you are to find a bed somewhere and get some sleep. Corrie will make you a hot negus and Tod will tell me all I want to know."

Orders were given for beds to be made up and aired, not only for herself and Corrie but for her men-servants as well, as there would be errands to be run to Dover Street and Manchester Square. Feeling for the first time that the weight of responsibility had been lifted from his shoulders, and with the promise that he would be roused should any change in Frank's condition make it necessary, Edward retired to his tent bed upstairs and slept dreamlessly.

Having thus descended on Sloane Street, Lady Chevening took no time in dismissing Edward's cook. "A drunken creature like that is no use in your kitchen," she told Edward severely as they ate their dinner on the second day of her stay. "Mrs. Flynn is going to send you Matilda Hookey tomorrow. She tells me she is excellent in the stillroom as well as in the kitchen, and is a steady, respectable girl. If she settles with you I daresay her brother will come back to you as head groom."

"Head groom? But Mamma, I have a groom already and Tod drives the carriage when I want it."

"Tod is an excellent servant, but you will need more than one groom now, Eddy. You will move from this horrid district into an establishment more in keeping with your position. For one thing," continued his mother before he could regain his breath, "you need a more commodious gallery for that collection of yours—especially now that it has attracted the attention of a certain important personage." Her eyes met his and the severity in them melted. "You stole a march on me there; I could have slapped Minnie for flitting off like that without breathing a syllable."

"But you understood my predicament, I hope, ma'am?"

"Of course I understood it, and angry as I was, I will admit that I was proud of you too." She stretched out a hand to him over the table. "I am afraid there have been times when I have not been as kind to you as I might have been, my dear. It is wrong for a woman to have favorites in her own family. But that is all over now." The thought of Vincent touched her mind fleetingly, and then she roused herself. "You have promised to help Tod wash Frank and get him comfortable for the night, so you must go."

"He has eaten nothing today," said Edward.

"He still has a high fever, but Corrie has made a syllabub and he will not dare refuse it if I am there."

It was two days later when Lucinda arrived in Manchester Square. She came on at once to Sloane Street, to be welcomed not by Edward, who, she was told firmly, had been sent out in his gig to take the air, but by Lady Chevening. Her ladyship took the girl into the little breakfast room that she had made her sitting room since she had been there. When Lucinda asked tearfully after her brother, she was told briskly that when she had rested a little, and had some wine and biscuits, she would be taken to see him. "But no tears, my dear," Lady Chevening added warningly. "If you are going to be a help to your brother there is to be no gloom in this house. Only cheerfulness, please. So dry your eyes and drink a glass of wine and do not look so sad."

Lord Crayne was also staying in Manchester Square, but he did not see Frank until the next morning, after he had spoken to the physician. That gentleman shook his head over his patient's fever, which appeared to be increasing with the passing of the days.

"In such cases, my lord, certain infections arise from the broken bones which one can do little to counter, except by extensive bleeding, and I fear that Mr. Crayne is no longer in a fit condition for such measures."

"You think my nephew may die?"

"I very much fear that possibility, my lord."

Lord Crayne had himself driven to Sloane Street. Taken to the sickroom, he stood for some time staring down at the invalid. He departed with a quiet word of thanks to Edward and his mother for their care of Frank, received by Edward in miserable silence and by her lady-ship with a cheerful counsel not to despair. There were occasions, she told his lordship, when even the most eminent physicians had been defeated by their patients' determination to recover.

After they had watched him climb heavily into his carriage, Lady Chevening sent her son out for a walk. Lucinda would be there shortly to sit with her brother, she told him, and if he met her with such a long face the poor girl would be frightened to death.

Edward was glad to be out when Lucinda arrived. He felt that her dislike for his family must by this time amount to detestation, and as he walked, scarcely knowing where his steps were taking him, his thoughts went back to Vincent and how, even from the grave, his elder brother appeared to be able to reach him and spoil his life as he had spoilt it all the years before he was killed.

In the meantime, having discovered that Sir William remained in Dover Street, Lord Crayne called upon him there. After a short conversation the two gentlemen visited a house in Bedford Square where Mr. Rick Delamere resided when he was in town.

Informed that he was at home, they said their business with him was urgent, and were shown upstairs into the young man's dressing room where his man was changing his slippers for boots before he went out.

"I have no doubt," said his lordship when the boots were finally fitted and the man had left them, "you may have guessed why we are here."

" 'Pon on my word I've not the slightest notion, sir." Rick laughed, but his laughter had a nervous ring to it.

"Have you not heard of the attack upon my nephew last month?" asked Lord Crayne quietly.

"Oh yes, indeed. A terrible business. I hope he was not seriously hurt?"

Herbert Crayne's grasp tightened on the head of his cane as if he would like to lay it across the young man's shoulders. He said, breathing deeply, "I have seen his physician this morning and there is a distinct possibility that he will not survive." There was an uncomfortable little silence and then Sir William said: "Fortunately the ringleader of his attackers was captured and he is ready to turn King's Evidence. His name is Brodie; I believe he is your servant, sir?"

"Oh no." Rick Delamere's eyes were wary now. "I dismissed him some time ago."

"But he was your servant when the attack was made upon Frank Crayne, and he will say in Court that you paid him—not to attack Frank Crayne, but to attack my son Jasper. He will also be prepared to state that the accident that killed my eldest son last August was caused because you deliberately pushed his horses into a fence that you knew to be rotten. The charges to be brought against you, Mr. Delamere, will be those of manslaughter, and if Frank Crayne should die—murder."

"You cannot convict me of these things on the trumped-up evidence of one servant." Rick attempted to bluster, and then seeing the determination in their faces suddenly gave in. "Very well," he said recklessly, "I admit that I did cut across Vincent's horses so that he would have to drive into the fence. He had boasted openly about the superiority of his horses and his curricle to mine, and I do not allow my friends to go to the horse-dealers and coach-makers that I have recommended and serve me in such a fashion. I did not, of course, mean to kill him.

As for Frank Crayne, it was all a mistake. I told that fool Brodie to watch for Jasper because he had humiliated me in front of a large concourse of people, and that I found unforgivable. I am a proud man, Lord Crayne."

"I am doubtful if you have a great deal to be proud of, Mr. Delamere, but if you wish to preserve that pride, Sir William and I suggest that you leave England tonight and that you do not return."

"Leave England?"

"If you do not, tomorrow morning you will be arrested and charged and you will face deportation at the very least," said Sir William. "It would be more pleasant to travel in a manner of your own choice than in the hold of a convicts' ship."

As they walked back to Dover Street he remarked thoughtfully to Lord Crayne, "So Jasper was right about that accident, and the rest of us were wrong, and I always took him for the fool of the family."

"Even fools have their moments of wisdom," said his lordship.

The two gentlemen were not surprised to see a paragraph in the *Courier* a few days later stating that Mr. Rick Delamere had left England for his father's sugar plantations in Barbados and did not anticipate returning for some time.

In the midst of her anxiety for her brother, Lucinda could not fail to notice the strained kindness with which Edward greeted her on the occasions when they met in his house. She was as wretchedly relieved as he was when the walks on which his mother insisted took him out of the house.

Every day when she visited Sloane Street she found

some added thoughtfulness on the part of Edward and his mother for her comfort, as well as that of her brother, and the care they both showed for Frank made her feel ashamed of the way she had abused his family in Brighton. But she had no opportunity now to explain or to apologize: the fight for Frank's life kept them all too occupied to spare time for their own feelings.

Whether it was the special food ordered by Sophia and cooked by Matilda Hookey—the bread jelly, the veal broth, the fresh eggs beaten up in milk and brandy—or whether it was the daily care with which Edward and Tod washed the patient from head to foot every morning in tepid water, or whether it was simply Frank's stubborn constitution that was the real cause for his recovery, nobody would ever know. One afternoon when Edward returned from a ride in the park he found Lucinda in the gallery upstairs, her fashionable bonnet thrown on the floor as she sat with the little bronze horse in her hands, weeping softly.

"Lucinda!" He came to her quickly, utterly dismayed. "Frank—is he worse?"

"Oh no." She shook her head, put down the little horse and dashed away her tears with the back of her hand. "Don't tell your mamma that I've been crying. Indeed I did not mean to cry—it is only because I am so happy. Edward, the fever has left him at last—Frank is sleeping like a child."

"To cry because you are happy is a very curious thing," said Edward, but indistinctly, because in some strange way she was in his arms, and her head was on his shoulder, and his hand was stroking her hair, while he murmured all the endearing things he had longed to say ever since her earring had come loose in the Edgecombe library. "My lovely

Lucinda—you shall cry all you want and I will see that my mother does not scold you. Indeed I would not be surprised if she had shed a tear or two herself in secret. My mother," he told her seriously, "is a very remarkable woman."

"Your mother, Edward, is wonderful. I think I love her almost as much as I love you." And when she said that he knew that the shadow of Vincent had finally been removed from his life.

Edward's parents were delighted to hear that Lucinda was to be added to his Collection, and even Lord Crayne admitted that she could not have done better.

When Frank was able to be moved he was taken to Chevening, because Sophia considered Buckinghamshire to be too cold for an invalid. Lucinda went with him, and Lord Crayne was welcomed there too, sitting beside his heir with much business talk and playing chess with Liz in the evenings.

Her parents were amused by the friendship that had developed between their youngest daughter and Frank's uncle. "If it had been Maria now, I could understand it," Sophia told Lady Stroud. "But Liz is scarcely out of the schoolroom, and she bullies the poor man and orders him about as if he were Frank's age."

Certainly their children continued to surprise Sir William and his wife that autumn. Jasper, full of remorse because of what had happened to Frank as a consequence of his besting of Delamere, was slightly cheered to know that he had been proved right about Vincent's accident. His boredom with his army career increased, however, and when his father's youngest brother, Admiral Chevening, came to London for Edward's wedding and advised his nephew to sell his commission and join him on his flagship as a junior officer, he jumped at the chance.

This was not the only shock in store for the Chevenings. Scarcely a fortnight after Edward and his bride had left for their honeymoon at Edgecombe, Liz announced her engagement to Lord Crayne.

"I told Will I could not understand how he could give his consent," Sophia told her sister-in-law, who was staying on at Dover Street for a little while after the wedding. "But he said he could not do otherwise. Crayne is nearly his age and old enough to be Liz's father, but he dotes on her and she has him under her little finger—the minx."

Lucinda, however, wrote from Edgecombe to say that she would adore to have Liz for her aunt, and Frank did not seem to be in the least put out with the engagement either. He had come to London to give his sister away, and was now well enough to return to his bachelor apartments in Manchester Street. One morning, meeting Lady Stroud in the park where she was taking a walk before returning to Chevening the next day, he told her that it was a great relief to him to feel that there might in the future be other heirs to Crayne than himself.

"So my brother and sister-in-law will have only one child left at home," Lady Stroud said thoughtfully. "Maria."

"And she declares she is going to be an old maid," Frank said, smiling. "She is talking of going into caps."

"Never! Why, she is not yet twenty."

"She says that every family should have a maiden aunt, and I believe she means it too." He caught a sympathetic glance from under Lady Stroud's bonnet and gave a wry little smile. "You are perfectly correct—I did ask her. But she told me she had given her heart to a bad and unscrupulous man, and although he nearly killed me and certainly killed Vincent, he has only to write her a letter with the one word 'Come,' and she would leave England by the next ship bound for the West Indies."

"But I do not think he will write, do you?"

"No. She will wait for a letter that will never come, but in the meantime she will be a joy to her parents as they grow older, and a beloved aunt to their grandchildren. She is quite right in what she says, you know. There should be a maiden aunt in every family, and it will be a poor outlook for English families if the supply should ever dry up."

"And you?" she said, taking his hand. "What will you do?"

"Oh, I shall wait too," he said cheerfully. "I am a very patient man."

Mary Stewart

"Mary Stewart is magic" is the way Anthony Boucher puts it. Each and every one of her novels is a kind of enchantment, a spellbinding experience that has won acclaim from the critics, millions of fans, and a permanent place at the top.

☐	AIRS ABOVE THE GROUND	23868-7	$1.95
☐	THE CRYSTAL CAVE	23315-4	$1.95
☐	THE GABRIEL HOUNDS	23946-2	$1.95
☐	THE HOLLOW HILLS	23316-2	$1.95
☐	THE IVY TREE	23251-4	$1.75
☐	MADAM, WILL YOU TALK	23250-6	$1.75
☐	THE MOON-SPINNERS	23941-4	$1.95
☐	MY BROTHER MICHAEL	22974-2	$1.75
☐	NINE COACHES WAITING	23121-6	$1.75
☐	THIS ROUGH MAGIC	22846-0	$1.75
☐	THUNDER ON THE RIGHT	23940-3	$1.95
☐	TOUCH NOT THE CAT	23201-8	$1.95

Buy them at your local bookstores or use this handy coupon for ordering:

FAWCETT BOOKS GROUP
P.O. Box C730, 524 Myrtle Ave., Pratt Station, Brooklyn, N.Y. 11205

Please send me the books I have checked above. Orders for less than 5 books must include 75¢ for the first book and 25¢ for each additional book to cover mailing and handling. I enclose $_____ in check or money order.

Name_____

Address_____

City_____ State/Zip_____

Please allow 4 to 5 weeks for delivery.

B-1

Sylvia Thorpe

Romantic tales of adventure, intrigue, and gallantry.

☐ BEGGAR ON HORSEBACK	23091-0	$1.50
☐ CAPTAIN GALLANT	23547-5	$1.75
☐ FAIR SHINE THE DAY	23229-8	$1.75
☐ A FLASH OF SCARLET	23533-5	$1.75
☐ THE CHANGING TIDE	23418-5	$1.75
☐ THE GOLDEN PANTHER	23006-6	$1.50
☐ THE RELUCTANT ADVENTURESS	23426-6	$1.50
☐ ROGUES' COVENANT	23041-4	$1.50
☐ ROMANTIC LADY	Q2910	$1.50
☐ THE SCANDALOUS LADY ROBIN	23622-6	$1.75
☐ THE SCAPEGRACE	23478-9	$1.50
☐ THE SCARLET DOMINO	23220-4	$1.50
☐ THE SILVER NIGHTINGALE	23379-9	$1.50
☐ SPRING WILL COME AGAIN	23346-4	$1.50
☐ THE SWORD AND THE SHADOW	22945-9	$1.50
☐ SWORD OF VENGEANCE	23136-4	$1.50
☐ TARRINGTON CHASE	23520-3	$1.75

Buy them at your local bookstores or use this handy coupon for ordering:

FAWCETT BOOKS GROUP
P.O. Box C730, 524 Myrtle Ave., Pratt Station, Brooklyn, N.Y. 11205

Please send me the books I have checked above. Orders for less than 5 books must include 75¢ for the first book and 25¢ for each additional book to cover mailing and handling. I enclose $_____ in check or money order.

Name_____
Address_____
City_____State/Zip_____

Please allow 4 to 5 weeks for delivery.

Dorothy Eden

One of today's outstanding novelists writes tales about love, intrigue, wealth, power—and, of course, romance. Here are romantic novels of suspense at their best.

☐ AN AFTERNOON WALK	23072-4	$1.75
☐ DARKWATER	23544-0	$1.95
☐ THE HOUSE ON HAY HILL	23789-3	$1.95
☐ LADY OF MALLOW	23167-4	$1.75
☐ THE MARRIAGE CHEST	23032-5	$1.50
☐ MELBURY SQUARE	22973-4	$1.75
☐ THE MILLIONAIRE'S DAUGHTER	23186-0	$1.95
☐ NEVER CALL IT LOVING	23143-7	$1.95
☐ RAVENSCROFT	23760-5	$1.75
☐ THE SALAMANCA DRUM	23548-9	$1.95
☐ THE SHADOW WIFE	23699-4	$1.75
☐ SIEGE IN THE SUN	23884-9	$1.95
☐ SLEEP IN THE WOODS	23706-0	$1.95
☐ SPEAK TO ME OF LOVE	22735-9	$1.75
☐ THE TIME OF THE DRAGON	23059-7	$1.95
☐ THE VINES OF YARRABEE	23184-4	$1.95
☐ WAITING FOR WILLA	23187-9	$1.50
☐ WINTERWOOD	23185-2	$1.75

Buy them at your local bookstores or use this handy coupon for ordering.

FAWCETT BOOKS GROUP
P.O. Box C730, 524 Myrtle Ave., Pratt Station, Brooklyn, N.Y. 11205

Please send me the books I have checked above. Orders for less than 5 books must include 75¢ for the first book and 25¢ for each additional book to cover mailing and handling. I enclose $_____ in check or money order.

Name_____
Address_____
City_____State/Zip_____
Please allow 4 to 5 weeks for delivery.